S. Baring-Gou

John Herring
Volume 3

S. Baring-Gould

John Herring
Volume 3

1st Edition | ISBN: 978-3-75235-114-9

Place of Publication: Frankfurt am Main, Germany

Year of Publication: 2020

Outlook Verlag GmbH, Germany.

JOHN HERRING

BY SABINEBARING-GOULD

VOL. III.

CHAPTER XLI.

WHITE FAVOURS.

The weather had changed abruptly. The wind had turned north-east, had become rough and frozen, and whirled snow before it over a white world.

Eight days had elapsed, and the marriage ceremony had been performed in the chapel of Trecarrel. The Captain was not present at the ceremony: he was in bed, indisposed.

The carriage was at the door of Dolbeare to convey the bride and bridegroom to Welltown. A hasty breakfast had been taken. No friends had been invited. The journey was long, and the horses must be rested midway for an hour. The days were short, and there was no chance of reaching Welltown before dark. It was bad travelling over fresh snow, and along an exposed road swept by the furious gale. The horses stamped and pawed the snow, the post-boys were impatient. Herring was anxious to start. Mirelle was upstairs in her room alone. All the boxes were corded and in place. Then Orange, who was in the hall, called her cousin.

Mirelle appeared, slowly and uncertainly descending the stairs. Orange uttered an exclamation of surprise. 'My dear, you are still in white! You have not put on your travelling dress.'

'I did not know.'

'But what in the world have you been doing?'

She had been weeping and praying. Her eyes were red and full of tears, and there was that exalted, luminous look in the white face of one whose soul has just descended from heaven, as there was in the face of Moses when he came down from the Mount. In her white dress, with her white veil over her dark hair, and a bunch of snowdrops in her bosom, just as she had stood at the altar, so she was going forth into the stormy world—as white as one of the snow-flakes, as fragile, altogether as pure.

Her travelling dress was in the box, and the box was on the carriage. There was no help for it; the box could not be taken down and unpacked. She must go as she was, wrapped round with many cloaks.

She was reluctant to depart. She had not spent happy days in Dolbeare; but, nevertheless, she did not like to leave it for the unknown. The future was strange and feared. Orange and her mother had not been congenial friends, but they were of her own sex. What would become of the Trampleasures now? They were without money. She turned to her husband.

'Mr. Herring,' she said timidly, 'my mother and my sister, what of them?'

'Dearest Mirelle, that is as you like.'

'Oh, Orange! and you, Mrs. Trampleasure! Will you come and live with me where I am going? I entreat you to do so. Make my home your own. I do not think you will be happy here, where you have met with so many sorrows. And I—I shall miss you.'

She looked at Herring, asking with her eyes if she had done right.

This was not what he wished. Orange was not the sort of companion he relished for his wife. There was an indescribable something about her which he disliked. Then an idea struck him. He called Orange and Mirelle aside into the little drawing-room.

'Mirelle, everything I have is yours. You may dispose of all at your pleasure. I know what has happened here. Orange is engaged to be married to Captain Trecarrel; but, through the sad disaster that has taken place, her little fortune is lost. Is it your wish, Mirelle, that this sum should be made up to her? The loss of this fortune stands in the way of her happiness and that of Captain Trecarrel.'

Mirelle trembled, looked down for a moment, and then said, 'Yes, dear

Orange, it shall be so. All that sum which was to have been yours, but which was lost, shall be given to you. Be happy with Captain Trecarrel.'

Then Orange flamed up. Her eyes sparkled, her cheeks flushed, and she clenched her hands.

'Never, never!' she exclaimed. 'He deserted and insulted me. Never, never, will I take him.'

'Well, Orange,' said Herring, 'you do as you think best. The same sum that was lodged by your father in my hands in trust for you, to be paid over on your marriage, shall be placed in the bank in your name. If you can forgive the Captain, well, so be it. None will be better pleased to hear it than Mirelle and I; but if not, you will find a welcome at Welltown. I must not delay longer. We have a lengthy drive before us, and cannot reach our destination while there is light in the sky.'

He handed Mirelle into the carriage, and stepped in himself.

The post-boys wiped their lips—they had been given a tumbler each of spiced wine—they cracked their whips, and away whirled the carriage.

'Orange, Orange! throw rice!' called Mrs. Trampleasure.

Orange stooped, picked up a handful of snow, and flung it after them, in at the carriage window, and it fell over Herring and Mirelle, a cold shower.

But the maid was more vehement and strict in her adhesion to traditional usage. First one slipper—a red one, then another—black, whirled through the snowy air, and fell in their track.

'What are you about, Bella!' exclaimed Mrs. Trampleasure. 'That's my dear 'usband's slipper—that red one is, and the other is Sampson's.'

'Look!' said Orange. The red slipper and the black had fallen with the toes pointing in the direction taken by the carriage, and lay between the wheel-marks.

'Mother, it looks just as though the dead father and the runaway son were after them.'

Hark! what is that? A faint, low music, scarce audible, and when heard at once caught and puffed away by the frozen blast. Was that the wind, playing a weird æolian strain through the spines of the Scotch fir? But if so, strange that the vibrations should frame themselves into a strain like that of Ford's old glee:—

> Since first I saw your face, I resolv'd
>
> To honour and renown you!

'Come in, mother, the wind is cold. It freezes to the marrow.'

CHAPTER XLII.

THE SNOW BRIDE.

A wild road that which leads from Launceston to Boscastle, up hill continuously, for miles after miles, across barren moor unrelieved by rocks, studded at intervals by cairns under which dead primaeval warriors lie. In summertime the road is rendered tolerable by the distant views; the rugged range of Cornish tors, Brown Willy and Row Tor on the left; far away south the dome of Hengistdun, where the Britons made their last stand against Athelstan, and which to the present day is studded with the cairns that cover their dead. To the south-east the grand distant range of Dartmoor lost in cobalt blue.

But that road, on such a day as this, was unendurable. There was no

5

shelter whatever; not a hedge, not a tree; not a village was passed through. Llaneast, Tresmeer, Treneglos, Egloskerry, lie buried in valleys where trees grow and the sun sleeps on smooth greenswards. The road seemed to be slowly mounting into the skies, into the bosoms of the snowclouds which shed their cold contents over it. White favours! The horses were plastered with them, the post-boys were patched with them, the carriage encrusted with them, the windows frosted over with them. Mirelle sat on the east side; she tried to look through the glasses, but could see nothing but snow crystals.

Herring spoke to her, but conversation was impossible; the wind howled and beat at the windows, as with icy hands, striving to smash them in. There was no keeping the wind out; it drove in between the frames and the glass, it worked its way through below and chilled the feet on the matting.

The horses went slowly; the snow balled under their hoofs, and the post-boys had to descend repeatedly to clear their shoes. The road was no post-road, and no change of horses was to be had half-way. There was no choice, therefore, but to rest the jaded beasts at the wretched little tavern on the heath, called 'Drunkards all.' There is a legend to account for the name. A traveller came one Sunday to the pothouse, with its little cluster of cottages around, and saw the people reeling from the tavern to their homes in the morning. 'What!' he asked. 'Does no one go to church here?' 'No,' was the hiccuped reply. 'Sundays we drinks and drinks—here we be drunkards all.' He passed the same way one weekday, and found the cottagers staggering from the tavern to the fields. 'What!' he asked. 'Is no work done here weekdays?' 'No,' was the answer. 'We drinks and we drinks—here we be drunkards all.' Once again he passed that way, and it was midnight; but the road was encumbered with tipsy men and women. 'Does nobody sleep here?' 'Sleep!' was the reply. 'No, we drinks and we drinks—we be drunkards all.' And as he went through the churchyard of Davidstow, he saw tombstones inscribed "D.o.D.—D.A."; and when he asked the meaning, the sexton said, with his thumb over his shoulder. 'Them from where you came from; Died o' drink—Drunkards all.' So the hamlet got its name, and has kept it to the present day.

Herring begged that a great fire might be made up, and some smouldering turf was put on the hearth in the little guest room. Firewood was an unattainable luxury in this treeless waste; the only fuel was peat. The walls were whitewashed, the floor was slate, on which milk had been spilled, and was frozen. The turf had not taken the chill out of the air in the room when the hour for resting the horses was passed. Herring had ordered dinner, but nothing was to be had to eat, save fried ham and eggs, nothing to drink but hard cyder and muddy beer. Mirelle had no appetite. She sat in her white dress by the low fire, deadly pale, with dark rings about her eyes, shivering. She held her hands to the dull ashes, and thought of the sunny garden of the Sacré Coeur. How the bees hummed there, and the hyacinths, blue and pink, bloomed early and filled the air with fragrance, and against the wall gold-green glistening flies preened their wings, loving the sun, and happy basking in it.

'It is time for us to move on, dear Mirelle,' said Herring; 'we have only made half of our way, but the worst half is done. The rest is, for a part at least, down hill.' She rose mechanically. He wrapped the shawls well round her, but there was no warmth in the slender white form to be wrapped in. There was no colour in her lips, none in the transparent cheek, only the blue icelike veins in her temples.

He led her to the carriage; again the post-boys wiped their lips, this time of sour cyder, and cracked their whips. The wheels went round noiselessly, and the carriage was lost to sight in the driving snow. Not only did the wheels revolve noiselessly, but the footfalls of the horses produced no sound; the postilions were silent, and those within the carriage did not speak. Verily that might have been taken for a bleached phantom coach drawn by phantom horses, conveying phantom bride and bridegroom from the grave of one at Launceston to the grave of another at Boscastle.

Herring took Mirelle's hand. She made no resistance. He held it in his, hoping that his warmth might thaw those frozen fingers. He pressed them, but met with no answering pressure; the hand was possibly too numbed to feel.

Now ensued hedges. They saw a woman, head down against the snow, stalking along the top of one—the usual footpath in these parts, where the lanes are often deep in water. Here and there came walls, and here and there ragged thorns; then moor again, and then the carriage began to descend.

Mirelle held her breath. Darkness had set in already; the post-boys lit their lamps at a cottage that was passed, and through the windows could be seen the snowflakes falling as flashes of white fire, in the radius of light cast by the lamps. The steam of the horses was blown back and formed haloes.

Mirelle's hand trembled in that of Herring. She looked round at him. He saw, by the reflection of the lamp-lights, that her eyes were wide with fear.

'What is the matter, dear Mirelle?'

'That noise—that terrible noise!'

'What! the roar of the ocean?'

The thunder of the Atlantic filled the air. Driven before the gale, the mighty billows dashed themselves to dust upon the adamantine cliffs and flung their shivers high into the air. The roar was continuous, but with pulsations in it, as the wind rose and fell. It seemed to Mirelle as if she and Herring were drifting in the vast void where there was no earth, no creation, no planets, no light, no life, no God; in chaos filled with howling winds and thundering unseen forces that clashed purposeless and self-destructive. But worse still, to the outer answered an inner desolation. There also, chaos was. She was drifting in spirit in a void, without a hope, without an interest, without a purpose, with heart and brain dead.

The carriage whirled down a rapid descent, and the roar waxed louder, more hungry, more terrible. No rocks could withstand the weight of water hurled against them. The iron walls must yield before those Titanic blows, and all the world dissolve and sink beneath the angry, inky ocean.

'Will that not cease?' asked Mirelle, timidly.

'The waves can always be heard here,' answered John Herring, 'but, of course, only as a pleasant mutter in still weather.'

'At night—does it go on all night?'

'To be sure; the sea never sleeps. In time you will come to love the sound. It will be a lullaby, soothing my darling to sleep.'

Mirelle shuddered.

Lights were visible, twinkling below.

'There is a little town, Boscastle, lying in that glen,' said he; 'we shall pass above it on our way home.'

Home! The word conveyed no warmth to the heart of Mirelle. Home is a quiet nook in the sun, among roses and mignonette, with a kitten purring at your feet, and a blackbird singing out of a syringa hard by, and the white cap of Josephine seen through the kitchen window, and her pleasant voice singing a *cantique* of the Mois de Marie whilst she shells peas. Home! A cold house in a void world, without a bush or tree, without stillness, in the midst of blackness and storm, and with salt spray and the boom of breaking billows filling the air with bitterness and thunder.

A scream over the carriage. Mirelle cried out in an agony of fear at that Banshee note.

'Do not be frightened,' said Herring. 'That was a gull driven in by the storm. Poor Mirelle! you will be glad when we reach home. This has been a trying day for you.'

She could not answer. She did not think she would be glad to reach Welltown; she was indifferent whether she got there or not. It was all one to her whether she alighted in a cold home or went on for ever and ever thus in storm and snow. Would it not be best of all to be allowed to descend and lie down on the white bank, and wrap the white fleeces round her, and so go to sleep? Then, indeed, she would go home—to a home she knew, to a home peopled with dear friends, saints and angels, with whom she had spoken from early childhood.

The longest day has its ending. The carriage drew up at last at the porch door of Welltown. Herring sprang out; no lights were in the windows. He looked along the front of the house; all was dark. No cheering welcome of twinkling candles, of ruddy fireflash through the panes. He knocked loudly. Then Genefer came to the door with a stable lanthorn.

'What! Master John! Well, to be sure. I never thought it. The day were so wisht and wild.'

'Jenny,' said Herring, impatiently, 'open at once. Let me in; you knew that we were to arrive this evening.'

'The storm raged so bad, I thought sure you'd put it off.'

'Come in, dear Mirelle,' said Herring, greatly incensed, and led his bride into the porch out of the wind.

'Have you no fires lighted? Nothing ready?' he asked, angrily, of Genefer.

'No, Master John. It be bad luck to wed in snow and storm: snow cools love and wind blows it away. I reckoned you knew that well enough, and would have put it off till the sun shone.'

A cold reception. The hall dark; only a little turf smouldering on the hearth, giving out neither light nor heat.

Mirelle came in. She did not look round; she was stupefied. It was all one to her. She had not expected much, and was not disappointed.

Genefer put the lanthorn on the table and proceeded to light a couple of wax candles. Herring divested Mirelle of her dark wraps.

Then the old woman looked at her. In the large gloomy hall Mirelle stood like a spectral figure, illumined by the candles, the white veil hanging; over her shoulders and back.

'Lord of mercy bless us!' exclaimed Genefer, starting back. 'It be the same—the same! O God!—the same I dreamed! The Snow Bride.'

She looked at her with dismay, then raised her hands and said, 'That ever I should have seen the day! O Master John! Master John! But the Lord sends strong delusions on them whom He will bring to naught.'

'Go at once, Jenny, and get supper ready. Heap up wood on the hearth. Is there a fire upstairs?'

'I don't know whether there be—there was, to dry the rooms; but there be nothing ready. It be a thousand pities you cannot get it all undone, and, if it must be done, do it another day, when the sun shines and the air be plum' (warm).

'This is intolerable,' said Herring, now thoroughly roused. 'You are determined, Jenny, to drive me beyond the limits of forbearance.'

'The Lord ordains,' answered Genefer: 'what will be will be. There! I'll have the fire up directly. Now, Hender'—aloud, and with her head through the kitchen door—'look spry, and bring in a faggot, and clap it on the turves. Take the bellows,' she said to Mirelle; 'blow away at them turves, and they'll glow. I'll be off and get something warm directly.' But, instead of going directly, she stood in the door, and looked at Herring, and said: 'The sheep always goes before the wind. You may put them in a loo place, but they won't bide there: they go with the wind to where they will freeze and die. It be all the same wi' men. When the Lord blows, they goes before His breath to their destruction, and not all the wisdom of the wise will avail to keep them loo.'

'Would you like to go upstairs, Mirelle, to your room?' asked Herring.

She lifted her sad eyes to his face and nodded. He took a candle and led the way. The boards creaked as they went up the uncarpeted stairs, and the wind wailed through the staircase window, clinking the little diamond panes; the draught was so great that the candle was nearly blown out. Against the glass the snow was patched in masses, as though the window had been pelted with snowballs, and the white patches reflected back the candle-light.

Upstairs was a bedroom, above the hall, and adjoining it a small boudoir over the porch. There was a fire on the hearth, and the bedding was ranged as a wall round it, to be well aired. Some billets of wood were heaped up beside the chimney-piece, and these Herring put on. He plied the bellows, and soon a yellow flame danced up. The room began to look more cheery. It was a pretty room; Herring had thought much about making it pleasant. The paper was bright, with roses in sprigs over the walls, and over the window were sprigged curtains lined with forget-me-not blue.

'There, dear Mirelle,' he said, 'I will have the boxes brought up; and I hope, in half an hour, Jenny will have dinner ready for us. I am sorry for her neglect. She is a tiresome, self-opinioned old woman, but you will come in time to value her. She is a Cornish crystal—and rough.'

He did not leave the room at once, but stood and looked round it; he had not seen it before, since it had been done up, with firelight flickering and candles lighted. He was pleased, and said, 'It is pretty—is it not, Mirelle?'

She looked up wonderingly at him. What was pretty? What could be pretty in such a place?

He had lighted candles on the dressing-table and on the mantelpiece. Over that hung a picture of his mother—a sweet young face, with a pleasant smile on it.

'That is my mother,' he said; 'she is looking down on you out of heaven. This was her room: I was born in it, and she died here.'

In a corner, near the fire, was a little *prie-dieu*, and over it a crucifix. Herring had procured that, because he made sure it would please Mirelle; but she did not observe it. She was cold, and crept near to the fire.

'I should like to show you the boudoir. I have done it up very nicely for you.'

'Oh, not now! another time.'

'Very well, Mirelle. I will go and hasten Genefer.'

He left the room, a little disappointed that no expression of pleasure had escaped her on seeing how he had thought and prepared for her. Then he

12

descended to the hall to stimulate Genefer to activity, and to see to his wife being given her boxes immediately.

More than half an hour passed before dinner was ready; when it was on the table, and the room was bright with candles, and a dancing fire was gambolling through a faggot of dry sticks, Herring went upstairs to call Mirelle. He found her sitting, still dressed in white, by the fire, looking into it, lost in a dream, with her hands folded in her lap, and tears on her cheeks. A little colour had returned to her lips, and the flickering firelight, reflected in her large dark eyes, gave them a fictitious life. She did not hear Herring enter, and when he spoke she started and shivered, as though frightened. She speedily recovered herself, and descended with him. She had removed her veil, but was otherwise unchanged in dress. The snowdrops in her bosom were crushed, and their bruised heads hung despondingly. Herring removed the bunch and put it in his button-hole. Mirelle could not eat much; she did not speak, except in brief answers to his questions. She was apparently thinking, and it was with an effort that she attended to what her husband said.

Genefer watched her intently. The old woman's face was grim and dissatisfied. She was respectful, and attended to her, but without the alacrity and cordiality in her manner that might have been looked for in an old family servant when welcoming to her home her master's bride.

When dinner was over, and Genefer had withdrawn, Herring said to Mirelle, 'Now, dearest, come into the ingle-nook, and sit on the settle. The great back will cut off every draught, and you will become warm there. I will bring my chair beside you.'

She rose, without answering, and took the place he indicated. The settle was of oak, dark and well polished, with the four cardinal virtues carved in panels above the heads of those who sat in it. It had stamped and gilt leather at the back, a little way up, and a crimson cushion on the seat. Herring thrust a footstool under Mirelle's feet, and, taking a chair, drew it near her.

'Dear Mirelle,' he said, 'welcome to your future home.'

'Thank you, Mr. Herring.'

'You must not call me *Mr.* Herring.'

'No, I know I must not. I will do my duty. I will call you by your Christian name. But you must not be angry with me it will not come at once. I will do my best, if you will have patience.'

'Mirelle!—nothing could make me angry with you.'

'Nothing?' Then she sighed and looked into the fire.

'Is there something troubling your mind?' he asked, unable to understand her manner.

'Yes,' she said, and looked up timidly at him, then withdrew her glance before his eyes; 'I will do my duty. You are my husband, and I must let you see all my heart. It is proper that you should. I will do what I know in my conscience to be right.'

'I will gladly look into that dear heart, and all I ask and hope is that I may find there a little sparkle of love for me.'

She shivered, and was silent again, still looking into the flames, broodingly.

'Dear, dear Mirelle,' he said, 'although you are now my wife, bound to me for ever, you have not yet given me, or received from me, a kiss. You have not once told me that you love me.'

Then she looked round full at him, with her large, sad, dark eyes, and rested them on him for full a minute without a word; but he saw that something was stirring in her heart. Then she said gravely, 'I respect you very much, John Herring.'

'Respect will not do for me. I want love,' he said with vehemence.

'I esteem you above all men.'

'That is insufficient. I will be satisfied with nothing short of love.'

'I do not love you.'

Those few words went like a bullet through his heart. He could not speak.

She saw that she had pained him unutterably. She went on. 'I am bound to speak the truth. I cannot lie; I cannot dissemble. What I say is true. I give you everything that is in my power to give. I am yours. I believe you to be the best, the noblest, the truest of men. But love——'

She slowly shook her head and sighed, and relapsed into looking into the burning wood.

His power of speech was gone from him.

'You must not expect too much from me,' she said; 'I will do my duty.'

'Duty!' he cried, and sprang to his feet. 'Duty is not what I ask for. I know you will do your duty—as an angel of God will do his duty. But I ask for, and must have—love.'

'I cannot, I cannot,' she said, in a desolate, despairing tone, and again shook her head.

'Why not? Is it so impossible to love a man whose whole heart is yours, who thinks of and cares only for you?'

'I would love you if I could! It is not my fault. I am willing, but I have not the power. I *cannot*.'

'Why can you not?'

She raised her large, dark eyes and looked at him, with a dull despair in them, and her lips quivered as she answered, 'Because I love another.'

That went like a second bullet through his heart, and rendered him speechless again.

'You are my husband. I know my duty. I am bound to conceal nothing from you. I am bound to tell you all that is on my heart. My love is for another. I cannot help it; you have nothing to fear. None can suffer from this as I do. I will try from day to day to deaden it. I will be true to you in thought as in deed. What I have promised, I will perform. But there it is—in my heart, burning, consuming. You could not put out that roaring fire on the hearth; it must blaze till it has eaten itself away. In time the fire here,' she touched her bosom, 'that fire, will have consumed itself and be white ashes, and the hearth cold. Then you may light another fire on it, but not till then.'

Herring had been standing looking at her, with one hand on his brow. Now he turned away.

'Are you angry?' she asked piteously. 'I felt in my conscience that I ought to conceal nothing from my husband; I knew that I was bound to tell you all. Are you angry?'

'I am in pain,' he said. His hand was on his heart. 'I am in deadly pain.'

'And I—I too,' she whispered, and her head drooped towards her lap, like one of her broken snowdrops.

Herring walked through the hall to the main door. There he turned.

'Mirelle!' His face was almost as white as hers.

'Yes, John.'

'God be with you. Good-bye!'

He opened the door. The wind tore in, and brought snow with it, and the thunder of the mad sea—mad that it had found a barrier which it could not demolish nor overleap, and in its madness tearing itself to spray.

Then the door shut, and Mirelle was alone.

CHAPTER XLIII.

HUNTING THE DEVIL.

Mirelle sat over the fire, looking into it. Had she done right in telling John Herring all her mind? She supposed that she had, and yet she was not quite sure. Her nature was so entirely frank, she had such a horror of concealment, that it had seemed to her a duty, an imperative duty, to lay bare her heart before her husband. She spoke out everything, without disguise, to her confessor, and the husband stood to her, she supposed, in much the same light. She would be guilty of a fraud, an impiety, if she allowed him to live with her without knowing the true state of her affections. She had thought this over a great deal, and she had satisfied her conscience that she was bound to tell him all. But now that the confession was made, she was frightened at the results. She had driven Herring from her. Whither was he gone? Would he return? Was it always right to speak the truth? Was not perfect openness the most refined form of cruelty?

Mirelle began dimly to see that she had acted unwisely; that she had been selfish in her desire to do her duty, and keep her own conscience clear. She owed a duty to her husband, a paramount duty, and the duty she owed him was to make him happy. In her effort to do her duty to herself she had run counter to her duty to him.

So she sat over the fire, in her white bridal dress, with her white face, and cold tears distilled slowly from her eyes.

Without, the wind raged, and splashes of snow were thrown, like mortar from a trowel, against the window panes. There was a red carpet on the hall floor, but the wind got under it, and it rolled like a sea of blood. She could see the first roller begin by the door and travel the whole length of the room. The curtains over the window swayed as though some one were in the embrasure stirring from side to side and pulling at the curtains to keep himself covered, and yet was seeking a place through which he might peep unperceived at the Snow Bride by the fire, melting away in tears.

The hall door creaked, and the latch, to her fancy, was tried; but no hand was there. It was the wind that thrust against the oaken boards and rattled the latch.

How the ocean roared! No doors nor windows could exclude that terrible all-pervading thunder. The sound was not in the wind alone, it was in the solid earth. It was not heard through the ear alone, it was felt by every nerve, for the foundations and the walls vibrated. In one of the hall windows was a cracked pane, and through it the wind screamed, and sobbed, and wailed. Were there ships at sea, this awful night? Were they near the coast? If so, there was no hope for the vessels, none for the crew. The stoutest ships must be broken against the iron cliffs, and the sailors dashed out of human shape.

There were souls drifting in that fierce wind and bitter cold—souls of drowned men on their way to purgatory and hell. What was that piping, and sighing, and crying at the window? Poor drowned souls peering in, and pleading to be admitted; poor souls still wet with the brine, shivering with cold, feeling their desolation, their nakedness, torn from the bodies they had so long and so happily tenanted; poor souls wailing and gnashing their teeth, because cast into the outer darkness and eternal cold.

A dog outside began to bark savagely. Had it seen the wan train of weeping souls sweep by? Then he lapsed into an occasional bark of distress, then was silent, then barked again.

What ailed the dog? The snow was drifting into his kennel, and he was cold and could not sleep.

There were rats in the old house. The cold had driven them in, and they were racing through the walls in quest of warm corners and of food. In one place glass had been put down to block a run; but the rats had broken their way through. Every rat that passed over the glass made it clink. They were between the ceiling and the floor overhead. One—two—three, one—two—three. One of the rats was three-legged, he had lost a foot in a gin. His footfalls could be distinguished from those of the other rats. He went slower than the rest, that old cripple; one—two—three, one—two—three.

Where was John Herring? What had become of him? Was he still walking in the snow and wind? Would he press on, thinking only of his misery, till, numbed with frost and weary of battling with the wind, he fell in the snow and slept his life away?

Whither would he go? What would he seek? Rest, and the lulling of the terrible pain from the wound she had dealt him. How could rest be got? Only in one way.

Then Mirelle sprang up, terrified at her own thoughts, and clasped her hands over her face to hide from her the horrible picture that rose before her fancy. She fell on her knees, faint with fear.

The three-legged rat had found a bit of tallow-candle end that had been thrust by a child through a knot in the flooring, and he skipped about on three paws, uncouthly, in an ecstasy of delight. But a rat with four legs came by and lusted after the candle end, and fell on the cripple, and bit him. He screamed with pain and for aid. Then other rats, sound in limb, ran to the scene, and, finding the cripple getting the worst of it, took sides against him, and bit and mangled him, he screaming with rage and pain all the while; and, after that, they divided the candle end between themselves, as their perquisite for having come to the aid of their four-legged brother, and left him the rush-wick, which he could not digest.

On the stairs was a clock—a very noisy clock, that ticked loud, and made a great whir before it struck the hours. This clock had dropped its weight, which fell with a crash the night John's mother died. The weight came down but once again, when Jago Herring, his father, died. A quaint old clock, with a figured face representing a drooping flower and a winged hourglass, and underneath the inscription—

> The flower fadeth,
>
> The hour runneth.
>
> Sic transit gloria mundi.

Twelve o'clock! Midnight had come, the hour when the dead are abroad.

Against the wall was a mirror. Mirelle was afraid to look in it. She knew that dead men peered over the shoulders of the living when they looked incautiously into the glass after twelve at night. What face might she see there? She took her handkerchief to put over it; the handkerchief was too small, and was, moreover, wet with her tears. She had a little shawl; she took that up—a black shawl—and went with it to the mirror, with head averted.

As she was engaged in hitching the ends of the shawl over the glass, she suddenly heard piercing cries, then howls and loud words shouted shrilly.

The shawl fell at her feet; she stood frozen to the floor; her heart stood still. The cries continued, waxing louder, more agonising; she heard feet racing along the passage upstairs, and then a man's voice, in gruff tones, raised in remonstrance. Then the door of her room was shaken, and again the man spoke. She could distinguish now what he said.

'Genefer! stand off. You may not go in and scare them wi' your screeching and devil visions.'

But the door was beaten open in spite of his protest, and the feet were audible rushing over the floor of the room. Then again a cry, a wail, and loud exclamations in shrill tones; and in another moment down the stairs came the feet, with sobs and moans, and Genefer Benoke burst into the hall, with a great cloak cast over her, her hair loose and flowing wildly about her shoulders, her large grey eyes wide open, and staring blankly before her, and both her hands extended in front of her, now scrabbling in the air, then expanded wide, with every finger apart. Her feet were bare.

'I see un! I see un! Look where he goes! Ah! thou foul devil! thou spirit of the bottomless pit! See, see! where he goes, the accursed one, with the smoke of the everlasting torment swaling round and round him!'

She stooped and picked up the black shawl, and lashed with it before her.

'Where goest thou? Do'y see un, Hender? Do'y see un? He be like a

20

black shadow with no sartain shape, stealing along, and now I sees a bit clear and then another bit. There be one fiery eye peer out, and now it be gone, and there shoots out another. Look in thicky corner, where he stands, and gapes and mows and tosses his arms. The Lord is my light and my salvation, whom then shall I fear? See, Hender! he has his fingers in his mouth and is drawing out the corners, out—wide—wider—like gum elastic, the whole width o' the room, and the fire comes out—it be the mouth of hell! Hender, Hender! see where he be writing on the wall, and the letters be letters of fire?'

Then she uttered a piercing shriek, and clasped her hands over her eyes, and buried her face in the black shawl.

Hender Benoke followed his wife.

'Come, come back to bed, Genefer. What do the devil mean by walking o' nights like this when it be freezing hard, and folks wants to be warm between the blankets? Come back, and if you must run arter 'un, run o' a summer night, ondeacent though it be—in your smock.'

'My boy! my John! O master, dear Master John! O the day, the day!'

'Come back to bed; you're frightening the young lady.'

'Her! her! the Snow Maiden that'll freeze the blood in the heart of un! Where be she? I cannot stay, it will be too late. I've a read the writing in fire. Let go, Hender; do not hold me back! I see the devil; he be making for the door, and I must after him, and smite him with the Lord's word. Come on, you—you!' She grasped Mirelle by the arm. 'It were you as brought the devil here to tempt us, and you must strive along of me to drive un, or he will carry the dear maister away.'

She made for the porch door, drawing Mirelle after her. Hender again interposed.

'Genny,' he said, 'you cannot; you must not.'

'Very well then—no!' exclaimed the woman, letting go her hold of Mirelle. 'No, no, it be none o' you can drive the devil, for you be an idolater,

21

and idolaters has their portion in the lake that burneth wi' fire for ever and ever. I must drive un with the Word of God. Run, Hender! bring me the great black Bible; quick, man. The devil be gone out at the porch door.'

She dashed to the window, tore aside the curtains, and cried: 'I see un, I see un on the snow, going like a puff o' smoke, and at every step he takes the snow glints white as a flash of moon. Bring me my black Bible, that I may pursue un, and catch un up, and smite un atcross the horns, and fell un like an ox.' Then she came into the midst of the room, and stood before Mirelle, and fixed her eyes sternly on her.

'Down on your knees, maiden,' she said, and pointed to the floor. 'Down on your knees if you know how to pray, and pray to the Lord for a soul, a poor, despairing, human soul as is brought to great temptation, and heaven or hell stands on the turn o' a hair. The Lord hath revealed to me that this night be fought the battle of Armageddon, and Apollyon and I must wrestle together for a human soul. Jacob wrestled with an angel till the break of day, and he would not let him go till he had blessed him. And I be called to wrestle, not wi' an angel but wi' a devil, and I will not let un go till I have tooked the soul that he be seeking out o' his hands. Down on your knees and help me if you can. Give me the Book.'

Hender had come in with the Bible. She snatched it out of his hands, and in another moment had slammed the door behind her, and was flying through the snow, with bare feet, and her black hair lashed by the wind, regardless of the cold and storm, holding the great Bible above her head with both hands, and crying after the black shadow that went like a puff of smoke before her, in whose treadings the snow glinted like flakes of moonlight.

Hender stood in the porch looking after her and muttering. But Mirelle was kneeling on the red carpet in the midst of the room, and the wind got in beneath and lifted and rolled this carpet about her, so that she seemed to be kneeling on a red sea.

All at once, Genefer stood still, threw up the Bible, caught it, and clasped it to her bosom. Both she and Hender heard a shot. A gun had been discharged; the report entered the room where Mirelle knelt, and she heard it.

'Glory be to God!' cried Genefer; 'he be driven back, but not by me. Sisera were slain by the hand of a woman, and it were revealed to Deborah that so it should be. So she went wi' Barak to the battle, for she reckoned that the woman into whose hand the Lord would sell Sisera were herself. But it were not so. Glory be to God! The devil be driven back, though not by me! I saw Satan as a stream o' smoking pitch run down Willapark and fall into Blackapit.'

Then she came quickly back, all her excitement over.

CHAPTER XLIV.

WILLAPARK.

Forth into the storm John Herring had gone. That day so desired had ended thus! He had gained her whom he loved—whom he had long loved, but only to know that her heart could never be his. He had taken the Snow Bride to him, and, as Genefer had warned him, she was about to chill him to death. No light would rise in those eyes for him; no smile come on those cheeks for him. Those lips would not meet his; that heart not beat for him. She respected him, but she feared him. Now he understood her conduct towards him through their engagement and that day. She stood in terror of him; she shrank from his love, because she had no love to give in return for it.

Herring could think of nothing continuously. The gnawing pain at his heart was too intense to suffer him to think connectedly. He was like one walking in semi-consciousness, staggering after a stunning blow, seeing nothing clearly, thinking no thought out. He did not know whither he was going.

He was without hat, he was without greatcoat. He had gone forth in his despair, without a thought of himself, what he should do, whither he should go. Did it matter whither he went? Wherever he went he must carry this pain with him. What should he do? He could do nothing, he could not staunch the wound that had been dealt him; the wound had cut too deep and had severed the main artery of life. There was no balm in Gilead for such a wound as that; it must bleed, bleed hope, energy, desire out of him. He cared nothing for life now. Life was a torture chamber, and the poor sufferer on the rack turns and cries out, 'Put an end to my agonies. Use the dagger, *la misericorde*!' What is

24

life, if granted, worth? After the rack, what is life with disjointed limbs and riven heart-strings? Who would receive as a boon so worthless a gift? No; in the torture chamber none ask for life, there but one desire is harboured, and that for death.

Herring had gone unconsciously towards Willapark, the headland that starts into the sea, gnawed half through by vast gulfs, in which the waves boil as in a cauldron. Willapark, white with snow, shelved up towards the sky; beyond was the void whence came thunderings and roarings, where nothing could be seen. So hitherto had he been going contentedly up his white way that led to heaven, expecting felicity at the top, and all at once he found himself at the edge of an unfathomed gulf, and a loved hand touched and thrust him over, and now he was falling into the awful void; whither he knew not, how it would end he only guessed.

By Blackapit was his little office, a small wooden erection; he could see it rising out of the snow. He had lived so much there of late, had slept there so frequently, that on leaving Welltown he instinctively took this direction.

He drew the key from his pocket and unlocked the door. Inside all was dark, and the smell was musty; the office had not been opened for some days. He shut the door, and went directly to his chair near the fireplace. There was, of course, no fire there, but that did not matter; he preferred sitting in the dark. How the gulls screamed around the house. The storm frightened them, even them, accustomed to wind and waves, and they cried and wailed as they fluttered disconsolately over the mainland. Perhaps they thought that in such a raging sea no fish would live, that all would be beaten to pulp, and their hope of food destroyed.

Herring seated himself in the chair; it was an arm-chair. He placed his elbow on the arm, and rested his throbbing temples in his hand.

This was the end. She did not love him, she loved another. Who was that other? That he did not know; she had not told him, and it did not concern him. All that concerned him was the one fact that she was not his. He had purchased to himself a precious heart, and when he knocked to be admitted he was told to abide outside, the key had been given to another.

He sat on in his wretchedness, not knowing how the time passed. He was becoming dead and cold in his chair, as Genefer had foreseen.

He stood up at last and struck a light. He kept tinder-box and candles in the Willapark office—tallow-candles they were—and he lighted one and placed it on his table.

Then he opened his desk and took paper, and a pen. His hand was so cold that he could not write. He tried to warm it with his breath, but in vain. He must write to Mirelle. If she had told him her secret, he must no longer conceal his—he must let her know that he had taken care of her fortune, and that it was now her own to do with it what she liked. Had she known that she was wealthy, she would never have accepted him, John Herring, now in purgatory, suffering for the wrong he had done her—a wrong done unconsciously and in good faith. She had taken him only because she believed herself to be destitute and dependent on his bounty. He had acted wrongly from the first. Light came to him, as to others, when too late to walk by it. Now he saw what the proper course would have been. If he mistrusted Tramplara, he should have confided all to Mirelle, and allowed her to choose her own trustee. But no! that would not have done, for, had the secret of the diamonds come out, old Tramplara would have claimed them as the legal guardian. He was bewildered; he did not know in what way he had acted wrongly, and yet what he had done, conscientiously believing he was doing right, had led to disaster—had landed him in a position from which there was but one escape. He had been to Mirelle a worse enemy than Tramplara. The trustee of her father's appointment had robbed her of the money intrusted to him; he, John Herring, the trustee of his own nomination, had robbed her of her life's happiness. Could he doubt for a moment that had she been free she would have refused him and have given her hand and fortune to the man of her choice? Now there lay before him no remedy save one. He had chained her to him, and whilst that chain remained she must suffer. Till it was broken, happiness was impossible to her. 'Oh, Mirelle! Mirelle!' the cry broke from, his heart. Here was bitterness past enduring, to be on the threshold of happiness, and to be thrust back; to have the cup at his lips, and to have it snatched from him and spilled on the ground.

He lit the fire in his grate, and warmed his fingers; he did not care for the comfort of the fire, he sought only to thaw his hand, to enable it to write. In his despair it seemed that there was but one course open to him—to restore to Mirelle the liberty of which he had deprived her. When able to write, he took the pen and ink, and slowly, with many pauses, gave her in full the story of the diamonds stolen by Grizzly Cobbledick from Mr. Strange's trunk, then given to him by Joyce. He assured Mirelle that he had acted as he supposed best, with no thought of reaping advantage to himself, certainly with none of gaining her by means of her own fortune. She would do him this justice. He confessed his mistake, and made the only amends in his power by restoring her the freedom of which he had deprived her. He did not date the account, but he signed it, and folded it. Then he made an abstract of all her money. He stated where the remainder of the uncut diamonds might be found, and what the amount of money was which he had received for those he had sold, and how he had disposed of this money. The room was his office, and his books were in it. He consulted them; and as he went over the accounts he recovered, to some extent, his composure; but his purpose never swerved.

When he had finished his task, he put the account with the letter, inclosed both in one wrapper, and sealed it. J.H. was his stamp; no arms, for he had no right to bear any.

Then he rose and went out, closing his door after him. He walked through the snow, which was thin on the headland, for the gale carried it away, and shook it into the sea or heaped it in the valleys. He could see, or he thought he could see, the distant lights of Welltown. Mirelle was not gone to bed yet; the light was red, shining through the hall curtains. What was Mirelle doing?

The snow had ceased to fall, and the air was clear of everything save

27

spray which was driven over the land in scuds. The headland shook under the blows of the ocean. On the left hand was that awful gulf, Blackapit, an almost circular well with sheer cliffs descending three hundred feet into the boiling foam and fury. He approached it; there was no rail, nothing to prevent any one from falling over. On a dark night, when no snow covered the ground, any one stepping astray would, in a moment, plunge into that horrible abyss never penetrated by the sun. At low water there was an inky tarn below, but now, through the narrow entrance, mountains of water beat their way, and when within tore themselves to froth in their agony to escape, and rolled back to the entrance, there to clash against another intruding billow. Then there rushed up into the air a white pillar of whirling foam that fell back again upon the contending surf below, unable to escape upwards. The roar of the raging water in this abyss was as the roar from the mouth of hell. There came upon Herring the thought of himself falling down that chasm, the hands extended, clutching at the rocks, and the nails torn to the quick in frantic effort to cling; kittiwakes, gulls, and skuas shrieking and dashing about him as he went down into that raging, ravening, thundering void. Rest there!—there—there! in that frantic turmoil, the very thought of which made a whirlpool in the brain! Herring sprang back with convulsive shrinking before such an end. No, he could not plunge down Blackapit!

He returned to his wooden house. It was warm and bright, and the sight of the fire and of the candle composed his nerves after that horrible dream of Blackapit. Over the fireplace was his gun—he had shot gulls with it from his window. On a summer day he had taken a boat and rowed about Blackapit and Welltown cove, and with a bullet killed porpoises. There were seals also in these bays. How horrible was the head of a seal, so human, rising straight out of the waves. He had never been able to kill one, the human eyes had unnerved him when he took aim.

He resumed his seat; his candle had a thief in it, a fungus, and burned dull. He snuffed the candle. Then he put some fuel on the fire, and looked musingly into it. He thought of how he had first known Mirelle, of her coldness towards him, how she had thrown away, or lost, his sprig of white heath. He remembered the very tones of her voice when she laughed at his name, Herring. He recalled her manner, as she scorned the idea of his being other than bourgeois. He recollected how she had cast reproach on the memory of her dead father, because he, being bourgeois, had dared to mate with her noble mother. And he had done the same thing—had taken advantage of her distress to tie her to him,—her the ideal of nobility, purity, beauty, to himself a humble yeoman's son, of no merit, and with few qualifications to attach any woman to him. His breathing was short; the pain at his heart was very real and physical. His head had been clear whilst he was working at the accounts, but now his brain began again to cloud over.

Then he stood up, and took down his gun. It was loaded with swanshot for the gulls. He had bullets in his drawer—for porpoises.

He drew the shot and went to his drawer; the bullets were not there. He turned over papers, and fishing tackle, and sundry odds and ends. He came upon a little book of sketches—how came they there? They were drawings he had made as a child of six and seven, very rude, and gaily painted with gamboge and carmine and Prussian blue. There was Noah's Ark, and the most marvellous beasts of all kaleidoscopic colours, marching up a plank into it. There was the Burning Fiery Furnace, and the three men being cast in at the top, comical little figures, with very little bodies, and very big hands and feet, all the toes and fingers extended. Herring remembered painting these pictures, at a table in a window, whilst Genefer was sewing, and his father was in the hall below, practising on his violin. He had painted these daubs in the little porch room, now done up in white and gold for Mirelle. No, the bullets were not in the drawer. He could not think where he had put them; his head was confused. He sat down again, with the gun across his knees. When had he last gone out porpoise-shooting? He could not remember. Not last summer, for he had been too fully engaged then at Upaver, and only making flying visits to Welltown, and then busy with the slate-quarry. As he sat thinking, the bunch of snowdrops Mirelle had worn fell at his feet. He had put them in his buttonhole when he removed them from her bosom, and now that he stooped they dropped.

He picked up the little bunch. Poor, bruised, broken flowers, crushed and withered like his hopes; pure flowers, white as Mirelle. They had rested all day in her bosom. He put them to his lips, and a great trembling like an ague attack came over him. If he had asked her to give him the flowers, would she have given them to him? Yes, but with a needle in them to pierce his hand. She had given him herself, but with herself his death-wound.

Now, all at once, he remembered where the bullets were—on a shelf in a sort of recess or cupboard at the foot of the bed. He went to the place and found them. He took one, dropped it down the barrel, and rammed it home.

'God forgive me,' he said, 'but there is no help for it. So alone can I undo the wrong I have done; so alone restore to Mirelle the liberty and the happiness of which I have defrauded her.'

He leaned his head on the barrel; the steel was cold to his hot and heavy brow. He rested it there some moments, thinking. Then he raised it, and the round red ring marked his forehead.

The gnawing pain was not there; there was trouble there, but the pain was in his heart, Then he lowered the butt end of the musket on the floor, and, leaning forward, placed the mouth of the barrel against his heart, and slid his hand down it towards the trigger. A sense of alleviation of pain, a foretaste of rest, came to him, from the pressure of the gun on his heart.

'God pardon me, it cannot be otherwise! May He be with her and bless her! Mirelle! Mirelle!'

He touched the trigger.

At that moment the door flew open.

'Maister! dear maister!'

With the start, the gun was discharged, but not through his heart; the bullet whizzed past his ear, and penetrated the roof.

Then ensued silence for a minute. Herring was leaning back, hardly knowing what had happened, and whether he were alive or dead.

The smoke filled the little room. As it cleared away, his eyes saw Joyce.

'Maister! sure you have frighted of me dreadful; but—I've a brought'y the stockings.'

He did not speak. He understood nothing.

'Dear maister! what be thicky gun for? Did'y think I were a robber, and you fired at me? No, no! I be no robber, I be come a long way. See! I ha' done it all myself. I sed as I would. I've a brought'y a pair o' stockings all of my own knitting.'

He remained speechless.

'Look!' she persisted; 'put thicky gashly gun away. There be no robbers here; I be your Joyce, your own poor Joyce. Look! the stockings be warm, of lambswool, and vitty, and I did knit mun every bit and croom myself.'

CHAPTER XLV.

'KINKUM-KUM.'

'It be warm and comfortable in here,' said Joyce, looking round her. 'Surely, I used to think it snug under the Table when the winds were loud; but there us had always a door open for the smoke to go out at. There were no chimney there, and there couldn't be none, for because of the great stone overhead.'

Herring put his hands to his brow. He was dazed. He could not understand Joyce's presence there and then.

'What a mighty long time you've a been away from West Wyke, maister!

But, sure, I have been away a bit too. I've a been with Farmer Facey to Coombow. I sed I'd go to 'n, and work out the hire of the waggon as brought you home after you were nigh upon killed by Cap'n Sampson Tramplara, and I did it. I went there, and I were there two whole months by the moon. Both Farmer Facey and his wife sed I did more work than two men. But, sure, this fire be beautiful. I've a been out in the snow and wind all day, and the most of the night too.'

Herring looked inquiringly at her.

'Where have you come from, Joyce?'

'Where have I come from? Where else, sure, but from West Wyke. I be come to look for you, and to bring'y the stockings I've a knitted. I sed I would, and I've a done it.

'I do not understand, Joyce. From West Wyke?'

'Sure-ly.'

'Not to-day, and in this storm?'

'I've not done this all in a day once for all, but I've been a foot all to-day, I can tell'y. It were hard walking. But see——' she held out her feet; they were stockinged and shod. 'Bain't that vitty' (tidy), 'and bain't I peart' (smart)? 'You should ha' seen mun, though, when they was new and beautiful; but I've a been so stogged in snow that they be now wetted through and through, and all their beauty washed out of 'em.'

'You have walked here?' Herring was coming out of his dazed condition into one of wonder at Joyce.

'Sure I have. I'll tell'y all about it, but I must sit me down by the fire; I be that stiff and tired I can scarce stand.'

'Joyce, what is the meaning of your coming?'

'I'll tell'y all right on end from beginning till now. I sed I'd a been working for Farmer Facey to Coombow.'

32

'What for?'

'Did you not hear me say it? He lent his waggon to dray you home to West Wyke, after you was nigh upon killed.'

'Well, what then?'

'Sure he wanted to be paid for it. There were a waggon and two horses for a day, and there were that boy, Jim White, along of them.'

'Why did you not tell me? I would have paid.'

'No,' answered Joyce, 'it were I as had the care of you. I sed I would do that, and I did it. I went and worked out the hire of the waggon and of Jim White myself.'

Herring looked at her with amazement.

'I cannot allow this,' he said.

'It be done,' she said, with an air of triumph. 'It be paid and all; I paid with my arms, by work; and the farmer sed I worked better than two able-bodied men, he did. And Farmer Facey's wife, her were a good un; her larned me to knit. It came about so. When as first I went there, I were that shy of going under the hellens, I thought I'd smother; so I sed I'd lie in the linney, and I did lie there a night or two. It were comfortable in the straw. But at last I seed the woman knitting stockings, and I sed I wished her'd larn me that; and her said her would if I'd come inside of the evenings—it were late in the fall, and the nights were long. Well, I were that set on larning that I did; I went in. I sed to you as I'd knit your stockings, and I've a done so. See, there they be. That Jim White were a worrit. If he'd a let me alone I'd have larned a deal faster; but I larned at last, I did. It wern't so bad and spifflicating after all in the house by the great fire. The smoke didn't fill the room; her went right on end up the chimney. Maister! when I were larning to knit stockings. I were that set up I thought I wern't like a savage no more as I used to be, but were dacent like other folk, and I found like that I could abide and breathe under hellens. Miss Cicely would hev taught me to knit, but I couldn't wait. I had to go to Coombow and work out the waggon and Jim White. I worked mun all out, and the farmer sed I were better to he than two labouring men. When I comed away at last, Mistress Facey her gived me thicky stockings, her'd a knit mun herself, and thicky shoes, they be brave and beautiful. Her gived them to me, and would take nothing for 'em. I didn't reckon much of 'em at fust, but I sees now I couldn't have walked here with bare feet in the snow. So they be good for more than to look to.'

'Why have you come here?'

'I've brought you the stockings I've knitted. I sed I would, and I've done it. You never came nigh to West Wyke for a long time, and Miss Cicely were lost to know what had become of you, and the old Squire be took worse; and I'd done the stockings, and I thought as you'd never come to see 'em. One day when the Squire were very bad, Miss Cicely comed to I, and said as how her wondered why you never came, and as how her wished you could know how the Squire were, and that he were axing every day after you. Then I sed, the stockings were done, and as you didn't come for mun, I'd carry mun to you. Her told me where you lived. I were to go right forward to Launceston, and there to ax my way to Boscastle. So I sed I'd go, and I'd take your stockings. The wind were up and there were going to be ice and snow, and you'd be wanting them to keep your feet warm. So I came.'

'But, Joyce, how did you find your way here, to this house?'

'I came about dark to Boscastle, and I went about and inquired after you, and some sed they didn't think you was here, and some sed, if I wanted to find you, I must go to the office, you were there mostly, and always of nights; and they gave me directions, and so I came.'

'But, Joyce, it is now past midnight.'

'I dare say it be. I couldn't get in at the door when first I found the little house, and tried, and there was no light in the windows, and I thought you might not be come yet, and I'd wait about a bit. So I waited on the lew side, but the wind were so wild, and the snow drifted, and I were forced to go away. But I came again after a while, and still the door were fast. So then I thought I'd go and find a haystack or a linney, where I might sleep, and I'd come again in the morning. But I rambled about for miles, and never found nothing of a place where I might lie. I got to one house, where there were lights in the windows, but a dog began to bark, and I were feared he might bite me as Farmer Freeze's dog had bitten and tore me—you mind that time as I hearkened to the hooddoo,—so I didn't venture into the shippon but comed away, and then I don't know exactly where and for how long I wandered about, but at last I saw a light here, and I found my way back to the office, but I had rare tumbles and climbings over walls and into ditches. However, I have found you here to last, dear maister, and I be glad, I be glad.'

'Good heavens, Joyce! is all this true?'

'Sure-ly. Did I ever tell you a lie?'

'Since when have you been afoot?'

'I started afore light, I reckon about five o'clock.'

'My poor, poor Joyce!'

'I be none so poor now. See my stockings and shoes! And do'y look here what a sight o' brave clothes I have, as Miss Cicely gave me.'

'Have you had anything to eat?'

'Sure. A woman at a cottage gave me some bread and a bowl of skimmed milk.'

'When?'

'I reckon at noon.'

'Twelve hours ago. Have you had nothing since?'

'No; I couldn't wait when I comed to Boscastle, I were that longing to get on and find you.'

'Joyce, you must be starving.' He sprang up and went to the cupboard, the same whence he had taken the bullet. A week ago he had a loaf and some cheese there. The bread was stale, but still it was edible. He brought it out, with the cheese and a knife.

'Joyce, off with these soaking shoes and stockings. Sit down at the table and eat what you can. I will get you something warmed over the fire to drink as quickly as I can.'

The thought of what Joyce had gone through distracted his attention from his own misery. There were others in the world beside Mirelle, others demanding his consideration and sympathy.

'The Squire be took cruel bad,' said Joyce, 'and Miss Cicely be very desirous to see you, and that you should come to the Squire. There be Upaver mine. Squire have a looked after things so long as he could, but there be nobody to do that now.'

'What is the matter with Mr. Battishill?'

'I dun know, but he be cruel bad; and the mistress were looking along the Okehampton road every day, and hoping as you would come. You've been such a long, long time away, and us can't get on without you no ways, that you knows very well.'

He was a help to some. His presence was desired by some. Only to Mirelle he was unwelcome.

'Be this house yours?' asked Joyce, looking round. 'I won't say but her's comfortable wi' fire and can'l and all sorts; but her's none so big as West Wyke, and not such a wonderful sight bigger than the Giant's Table. I know when I gets back, Miss Cicely will be asking of me about it; what sort of a place her be, and whether her be big or small, and built of stone. Her's all of board, just like some of them places they runned up to Ophir, where the gold was. But that be all tore abroad now.'

Poor girl, she was hungry. The bread was hard as biscuit, but she ate it eagerly. Herring gave her some hot wine and water.

'The old Squire be axing after you the first thing in the morning. And he do fret wonderful for you. Miss Cicely do say it be like a child wanting his nurse. He be gone a 'bit tottle' (foolish), 'I reckon.'

'I shall go back to West Wyke to-morrow, Joyce.'

'O glory rallaluley! I be glad. I'll have a wink of sleep, and then I'll be fresh as a buttercup to go wi' you. I may go along of you, mayn't I now, maister dear?'

'Yes, Joyce. You shall not walk, you shall ride.'

'I rided once afore wi' you,' she answered, 'but you know nort about that. It were when you were nigh upon dead, and I held your head in my arms all the way, and you never waked but once, and that were on Sourton Down, and then you held out your hands, entreating like, and cried something, and that were all, and never spoke no more.'

'What did I cry out?'

She looked steadily into his eyes, and said in a low tone, 'Mirelle.'

He covered his face, as a spasm contracted his heart. Joyce had touched too recent a wound for him to endure the touch without shrinking. Joyce saw that he was in pain. She went to him, and, kneeling at his feet, drew his hands away from his face, and looked into it; then shook her head.

'Her don't belong to you yet then?'

'No, and never will.' He spoke with bitterness.

'You be changed, maister dear. I never seed you afore like as you be now. You look just about a score of years older than what you was once. Is it the Whiteface has done it, or what be it, maister darling? Tell your own Joyce, and see if her won't go through ice and snow to serve you any day, if her can.'

'You can do nothing for me.'

Still she looked at him, holding his hands, trying to read his secret in his face, with eyes full of earnestness. Then, suddenly, there came a revulsion in his thoughts.

'God forgive me for what I have said! You do nothing for me!—Joyce, dear Joyce, you have done for me this night more than you are aware of. You saved my life once before, you have saved my life again to-night, and something more than my life.'

She did not understand him. How could she?

'Maister,' she said, 'put thicky gashly old gun away; it frightens me.'

He rose at once and obeyed, putting the gun back in its old place on the crooks.

'You be coming back to West Wyke?' she asked.

'Yes, to-morrow.'

'You'll be better there. There the old Squire be fond of you, and you be so kind to me; and there be Miss Cicely, too, her's a pining likewise, acause you be so long away; and there be I,' she looked down at his feet, 'knitting stockings as fast as I can knit for you. If I can do nothing more, I can do that.'

'Oh, Joyce! Joyce!' He could say no more, his heart was full. Here at Welltown—wretchedness, coldness, repulsion; there at West Wyke—not happiness indeed, but rest, warmth, and love.

'And, maister dear, you'll larn me the kinkum-kum. I wouldn't let Miss Cicely larn me. Her began to laugh when I said kinkum-kum. But when I were bad wi' my broken arms, and I asked you to say it, you didn't laugh, but you tooked off your hat and said it as good as a Methody. And now, I'll tell'y, that night when I drayed you out of the road into the wood, and thought you was going to die, and I didn't know what ever to do, I got such a pain here,' she put her hand to her heart, 'as I could scarce abear it. And then I went down on my knees, just the same as I be now, and I put up my hands over where you lay, and I cried that same kinkum-kum, and him as I knows nort about, he heard me, and he did what he could, I reckon. He made you better, and he set my pain and trouble at rest. There, maister darling, I can see you be in pain and trouble now. Just you do the same; go down on your knees, and

38

say the same right on end, and the rest from pain and trouble will come sure-
ly.'

'Joyce!'

She was still looking in his face, desiring something, with a great distress
in her eyes. Now, a smile broke in her eyes.

'O rallaluley!' she exclaimed. 'Your face were at first like Cosdon when
hard frozen, but now the springs be breaking.'

The lines in his face had softened, his lips quivered, and his eyes filled.
Then, all at once, he fell on his knees beside Joyce, and held up his hands as
she had taught him, and said in broken tones and slowly, 'Our Father.' Joyce
repeated the words.

'Which art in heaven—hallowed be thy name.'

Joyce still followed. 'Thy kingdom come.'

The storm had passed away, almost suddenly. The clouds had broken; in
the west the moon hung unveiled, and cast a ray of purest silver into the little
room, and bathed in her stainless light the poor savage and the young soldier,
kneeling and praying together.

CHAPTER XLVI.

A BAR OF ICE.

Next morning John Herring returned to Welltown. He was a changed man.
His lightheartedness, his simplicity of character, were gone for ever. Hitherto
he had been a big boy, with buoyant spirits and with a belief that the world
was a paradise. He was a man now, seeing life before him as a sad desert that
must be tramped over, where he must meet with suffering, and count himself

happy if, at long intervals, he reached and could rest by a brackish pool. The world is no paradise, it is a vale of Sodom, where the pits are bitterness and the rivers brine. It is no playground, it is a convict establishment. It is a theatre in which all act tragedies, and the lookers-on mistake them for farces.

Herring had spent the remainder of the night by his fire, revolving in his mind what must be done. Joyce slept soundly on his bed in the corner, tired out with her trudge through the snow. Herring had made her take off her gown, and had thrown an old fishing coat of his over her. Though he sat over the fire thinking of his own future and Mirelle's, he cared also for Joyce's boots and gown and stockings, that were drying by the stove, and turned them, and took thought that they were not burnt.

In the morning he sent Joyce into the village of Boscastle to detain the chaise in which he had come to Welltown the previous evening. Then he went to see Mirelle once more.

He was, as Joyce had observed, greatly oldened and altered. One night had worked the change in the outer as well as in the inner man. There comes a time to all when the rose-coloured spectacles must be laid aside for those of blue glass. The time comes sooner to some than to others. It had come now to John Herring, and the aspect of everything was changed to him.

Mirelle was unaltered. She was pale, indeed, but that was her usual complexion, and her eyes were red, but they had been red the day of her marriage. She was more collected than on the previous evening, and Herring was more composed.

He entered the house without Genefer perceiving him, and went upstairs to the little porch-room. Whilst he was in the hall he heard Mirelle's steps above, and knew she was there.

She did not seem surprised to see him. She received him with ease and gentle kindness, not as a husband, but as a friend. There was in her heart a sense of relief; she could speak with him on an understood footing, and she would not be subjected to demonstrative affection. Herring was prepared for this. She saw that he was looking worn and ill, but she made no remark. She was the cause of the change in his appearance, and she knew it. She regretted it, but it was inevitable.

Mirelle was dressed in a sober dark gown. Every trace of bridal white had been put away. When he entered, she was engaged on her trunks.

'Your jewels are here,' he said, showing her a secret drawer in a large old cabinet. 'I give you the key. Do not leave it about; though nothing is to be feared from Genefer or Hender, yet it is wise to keep articles of value under lock and key, and not to trust the key to any one.'

'They are of no value. They are paste.'

'I beg your pardon, they are not. I took them to a jeweller, who examined them. Some of the stones had been abstracted at some time, and replaced by artificial diamonds, by whom and when, I cannot, of course, say. I have had all these taken out, and true stones of good quality put in their places. The necklet and diadem are now perfect as at first.'

Mirelle was surprised.

'You think the set of diamonds was originally complete.'

'I am convinced it was so.'

'And that the stones had been removed and paste substitutes put instead into the sockets.'

'I believe so.'

'Then you do not think my father gave what was worthless to my mother?'

'I cannot suppose so. It is not likely. The pendant was tampered with more thoroughly than the rest of the set, because it was removable. Probably after that had been altered, one by one the stones of the necklace were removed. Some person in need of money disposed of the stones as the need came.'

Mirelle thought.

'Yes,' she said, 'I have no doubt it was done by Antoinette.'

'Who was Antoinette?'

'My mother's maid, who did everything for her. I am glad to think that my father was not guilty of a mean act. I thank you for clearing his memory from such a stain. Henceforth I shall believe that Antoinette was guilty.'

'So be it; and from henceforth I hope you will realise the necessity of keeping precious stones under lock and key. Show them to nobody unnecessarily, and, above all, show nobody where they are kept.'

They spoke to each other with perfect coolness and self-possession. Pyramus and Thisbe met and conversed with a wall between; John Herring and Mirelle were separated by an invisible wall, but it was one of ice.

'I have brought you, as well, the key of my office on Willapark. I keep there my accounts of the slate-quarry. Should anything from the office be required, the foreman will come to you. If not asking too much, I would wish him not to be given free run over it, and that you should be present when he wants anything. There are things there which I do not care for him to turn over, papers and accounts among which I do not wish him to rummage. You will do me this favour?'

'Certainly. Are you going away?'

'I am going away for a while. You know that I am working a valuable silver lead mine on the borders of Dartmoor, and it must be looked after.'

Why did he not say where it was—'near West Wyke? where you and I first met, where your father died?' He did not say this, because it would be painful for him to say it, and for her to hear it. The name would call up recollections they must endeavour to crush out of their minds.

'You will return again?'

'I will come back to see how the slate-quarry progresses. I had purposed building a breakwater, but I shall not now carry out this purpose.'

'Why not?'

'The lead mine is sure to engross nay time and attention. I shall be here but little. My interests will be centred in the silver lead.'

'Very well.'

'I shall provide for your comfort. You will have, as before, your own account in the bank, under the same name, Mirelle Garcia de Cantalejo. You will draw from the bank what you require.'

'I thank you, Mr. Herring. You are very kind.'

'You will do with the money what you like; you are entire mistress of it. You will pay for the expenses of the house from it, and keep what company you like. There are not many neighbours, but such as there are will call, and they will be hospitable to you, and glad to receive hospitality from you. I dare say you will require additional servants. Genefer——'

'I beg your pardon, I do not wish to have that woman in the house. She frightens me.'

'She is a worthy, devoted soul. You are sure to like her when once you have learned her value.'

'She frightens me; I thought I should have died of fear last night.'

'I cannot consent to her dismissal. She was my nurse, she has been with me from my birth, and loves me as if I were her own child. When I look back I see how her life has been devoted to me. Besides, the home farm is let to Hender, and he and she must live here: there is no other house for them, and the outbuildings are included in the lease. It is unavoidable. If I could have gratified you in this particular I would have done so, but I cannot.'

Mirelle became, if possible, colder. She bowed her head stiffly.

'Very well,' she said, after a pause, awkward to both: 'if it cannot be, I must endure this cross also. But I entreat you, do not say me nay to my next petition.'

'I will not. I would refuse you nothing, you may be very confident, but the impossible.'

'It will not be impossible for Orange and her mother to come here and reside with me.'

Herring took a hasty turn up and down the room. The request vexed him greatly. There was something in Orange he did not like, something in her manner towards Mirelle which made him mistrust her professions of affection, something—a coarseness of mind which he suspected rather than perceived, which he shrank from voluntarily bringing into contact with the unsullied purity and delicacy of Mirelle's soul.

'Is this also refused me?' asked Mirelle. Then her coldness giving way, the assumed stiffness yielding to her natural emotion, 'Oh, John Herring, do not be unkind to me! You have been so good, so much better to me than I deserve.'

'I—I unkind to you, Mirelle!' In a moment also his assumed coldness cracked, and the warm suffering heart showed its blood through the rent, as the black crust of lava that descends Vesuvius breaks, and the fire of the core is seen glowing between the rough edges.

'I tell you the truth, my friend,' she said. 'I will call you my friend; that you have been ever since we have known each other—that you are still.'

'Yes,' said Herring, regaining his composure, 'what I have been, that I am and shall be, your friend—nothing more.'

'I tell you the truth, that woman Genefer nearly killed me last night. I was sitting over the fire till late, after——' she hesitated.

'After I left you; yes, go on.'

'After you left me, after I had driven you away, my friend, my poor friend!' She looked up into his eyes piteously. He turned his away; he could not bear to look into the soul that was not his, that never could be his. She went on: 'After you were gone, I sat on till very late, thinking. I was unhappy, and I cried. I sat by the fire; you can understand, I was in trouble about myself and about you. After midnight I was roused by hearing the most dreadful shrieks and the rushing of feet along the passage overhead.'

'That was nothing,' said Herring, forcing a smile. 'My good Genefer has strange fancies that take her perversely at unsuitable seasons. She was only driving the devil.'

'But I cannot bear hearing the devil driven in the depth of the night, in a lonely house, in the midst of a raging storm. It will kill me. I have been very ill, you must remember, with a nervous fever, and it has left me weak and liable to be shaken by strange events. I fear that I cannot bear such an event again. I cannot stand much.' She looked now full of entreaty and helplessness —a frightened, feeble girl, in dread of strange things, she knew not what.

'That is true. I will see and speak to Genefer before I leave. I must give some explanation of, and excuse for, my hurried departure, and at the same time I will be peremptory with her on this point. She must not do such a thing again. If she wants to drive the devil, she must drive him in her own chapel.'

'This house is so lonely and cold. I must have some one always with me, some one whose presence will be a protection against fears, some one whom I can consult about matters that concern the house. I am wholly ignorant about these; I am only a girl just come from school, and come into a strange land. When I was at Dolbeare I slept with Orange, and I should like to have her here to sleep with me again. Then, if I heard noises in the night, I would cling to her, and she is so strong and so brave that she would protect me and revive my courage.'

'I do not like Orange.'

'May I not have her here? I must have some one, and I had rather have her than any one else.'

Herring again paced the room. A great repugnance to this proposal rose up in his heart: he had no real and reasonable grounds for it, but he had an

45

instinctive dread of the plan.

'You will not refuse me this,' pleaded Mirelle. 'See! I did not ask you for all those generous and kind things you have devised for me. But a man does not understand the feelings of a woman. You are strong and unable to comprehend my terrors. To you they are childish and absurd, but they are very real and serious to me. I only ask you this one thing—if Genefer must remain, let Orange come.'

He could not resolve to give his consent.

'Would it not be better if I were to find you a suitable companion, some lady, young, and, if you desired it, of your own faith?'

'How can I tell that she would suit me? There were many girls, my schoolfellows, at the Sacré Coeur. They were of my own age, and all were good Catholics, but with several of them I could not live, and with some I should not care to live. How can I tell that you would find me just the very girl that I should like? No, I know Orange. We do not think alike. She has not faith. She is older than I am, and though companions we are not intimates; but I know her, and she loves me; she has good sense and she can advise. That is all I want.'

'Was there no girl at your old school whom you would like to ask to come to you? You must have had some dear friend there.'

'Yes, there was la Princesse Marie de la Meillerie; we were close friends. But conceive! I could not invite her to this place of banishment, where there is not a tree nor a flower. This world here is not nature in flesh and clothing, it is the skeleton of nature, and it demands the enthusiasm of a geologist to admire such a country. My companions, again, were of the *haute noblesse*, and were not of the sort to become *gouvernantes* to young unprotected ladies.'

'No, I see that.'

'Moreover, who would come here, where you have a church picked bare to the bones of all that surrounds and sweetens religion? My friends are

46

Catholics, and love a living church, not one which is only bones, though the smallest of bones be preserved and *in situ*, and the entire skeleton be well set up.'

'I dare say it is so.'

'Then you will allow Orange Trampleasure and her mother to come to me. See you! they are at Launceston, and are left without money.'

'I promised in your name to place five thousand pounds to the account of Miss Orange.'

'Yes, I do wish that. But that is not sufficient. They are not comfortable at Launceston. It was there that they met with their great reverse. It was in that house that Mr. Trampleasure died. The people of Launceston suffered by the failure of the gold mine, and they will not forgive Mrs. Trampleasure and Orange, though only the old man and Mr. Sampson were guilty of wrong towards them. I know that Orange and her mother would like to leave the town, and go elsewhere, where they are not known. That also is a reason why I wish them to come to me.'

'Very well,' said Herring: 'if it must be so, let it be so. It is a compromise, and a compromise is never satisfactory. I retain Genefer and you Orange. Ask them to come here to you on a visit of a couple or three months —temporarily—not as a permanence, and only till they have made up their minds where they will finally settle.'

'I must accept this,' said Mirelle, with a sigh: 'you were so very, very kind to me *before*—now that we are married, you are only half as kind.'

'Do not speak like this,' said Herring, hastily. 'I am what I was before, a friend, nothing further—I can be nothing further.'

'You will be always my friend?'

'Always.'

He drew a long breath. His heart was swelling and likely again to rend the crust and show its fires. He conquered himself and held out his hand.

'You will find that one drawer of my desk in the office is locked; I keep the key to that. Everything else is open to you. Good-bye!'

'What, so soon?'

'I am going away in the carriage that brought us to this place yesterday.'

'Ah, well!—to the silver lead mine.'

'Yes.'

'What will be your address?'

'You will not need it.'

'Shall you soon return?'

'I do not know. Good-bye.'

They shook hands. Mirelle's lips trembled and her eyes filled. She bore Herring a sincere regard; she felt her deep indebtedness to him. She had treated him with great cruelty, and had caused him unspeakable suffering. This was a chilly separation. She felt inclined to say something better than 'good-bye'—that is, to say 'Stay.' But she could not do this.

They touched hands through the walls of ice that intervened, and that froze the word on her tongue.

CHAPTER XLVII.

WELCOME HOME!

The weather changed with the capriciousness proverbial in the West of England. There a week of continuous frost and east winds is almost unknown. No sooner has the snow been shaken over the hills than the sky repents of its cruelty, and brings a warm breath over the face of the land, before which the white mantle vanishes as if by magic, and the grass comes forth greener than before.

It was so now. The wind had changed after midnight, and a rapid thaw had set in. Herring returned to Launceston in the carriage in which he had left the day before. The post-boys had removed their favours, and the earth was putting off hers as well. Herring took poor Joyce back with him. When she came to Launceston, she desired to push on. She wished, she said, to go to Coombow and see Mistress Facey. Herring was obliged to remain the night in Launceston; he had to make the arrangements with the bank that he had undertaken.

He did not go to Dolbeare. He saw no one but the banker; and then he went on his way by coach. He did not pick up Joyce. Perhaps he overtook and passed her on the road without noticing her; his mind was full of his own troubles, and he had no attention to bestow on the road and those who were on it.

When he passed Okehampton his thoughts took a turn. The grand bulk of Cosdon rose before him. The soft glory of the evening sun was on it, the snow had not thawed off the mighty head, though it had gone from the valleys, except where drifted and screened from the wind and sun. The rooks were wheeling and cawing, they anticipated fine weather, and were thinking of overhauling their last year's nests. Valentine's Day, for birds as well as for maids and men, was only a month off. The rooks blackened a field, the worms had come out after the frost to enjoy the sun and soft breeze, and the rooks were enjoying the worms. 'Caw, caw!'

Then the guard blew his horn, and away they went, a rush of black wings, but to no great distance. They settled in a couple of oak trees, and waited till the coach had gone by. The coachman cracked his whip. That alarmed them more than the horn, it resembled the report of a gun, and they sprang into the air with loud remonstrances against a repetition of the St. Bartholomew's Day of last rook-shooting. 'Caw, caw!' They danced a minuet against the blue sky overhead, a minuet of incomparable intricacy. There be three things, said the wise king, too wonderful for me—the way of a bird in the air, the way of a ship in the sea, and the way of men and maids. The ship darts from side to side, tacking against adverse winds, aiming at a port which she seems to avoid; and the way of maids with men sweethearting, in the Valentine days, in sweet spring, is much the same, full of tricks and evasions, disguises and cross purposes, wonderful as the way of a ship, wonderful as the mystic dances of the rooks overhead.

The air was warm, the sounds were spring-like, the beautiful moor was glorified by the sun, setting in a web of golden vapour. The scene was familiar to Herring, associated with pleasant days. He got off the coach at the bridge over the Taw, that he might walk quietly up the hill and over the downs to West Wyke. Windows were glittering in the sun like gold leaf. There was one that was open and swinging in the light air. It flashed across the valley shafts of fire, welcoming flashes to the broken-hearted man toiling up the hill. In a thorn-bush the sparrows were chattering—hundreds holding parliament, all their little voices going together, and none attending to what the other sang or said. Lo! in the hedge, already, a celandine, the glossy petals as glorious as those flickering windows. A sense of rest after long trouble came upon Herring. He stooped and picked the celandine—January, and these bright

50

heralds of sunshine out already, come forth to welcome him home to West Wyke.

How soothing in his ear sounded the murmur of the Taw, rushing over the old grey granite boulders, breaking from the moor to run a quiet course through rich meadows and among pleasant groves. The gentle rush had a lullaby effect on the troubled heart of the walker. A very different sound this from the boom of the Atlantic against Willapark and the churning of the imprisoned billows in Blackapit.

A track led off the road to Upaver. How was the mine getting on? The track was well trampled and the wheel marks many; that was a cheering sign. Hard by stood a post which Tramplara had set up, painted white, with a board on it and a hand pointing moorwards, 'To the Gold Mines of Ophir.' Some one had scrambled up the post, scratched out the 'To,' and written in its place 'Damn,' giving thereby coarse but emphatic expression to the general sentiment. Herring smiled bitterly as he noticed this. Next he came to the cottages.

'Good evening, sir! Glad to see you home again.'

The speaker was a labourer returning to his fireside, his day's work over. Herring did not remember him, but the man knew him, and his tone showed pleasure.

Home!—was this home?

'How is all going on with you?' asked Herring.

'Well, sir, my missus hev given me another little maiden. That makes fourteen childer. Eight maidens and six boys, but we've a buried three.'

'You have your quiver full.'

'They bring their love wi' them, sir; and that, I reckon, you'll find when you've a home of your own, and a wife, and the little uns coming every year.'

Herring sighed.

'Good evening, sir. Here be my nest.'

'Good-night.' Then Herring went on—home? Before him was West Wyke, and the last glimpse of the sun was on it. The window of West Wyke it was that had flashed the welcome to him.

The old ash trees, the old gateway with the grey owls, the old chimneys, the old ivy-mantled porch, the old firelight flickering through the hall window. A moment more, and the old welcome.

With an exclamation of delight, Cicely sprang from a stool by the fire to meet him, as he entered without knocking; entered as he would to his home. He was no stranger, to knock and ask for admission. He went straight in, and in a moment felt that he ought to have more hands than two to give to those who grasped them.

The old Squire and Cicely held him.

'Oh, John, dear cousin John, you have come at last!'

'John, John, I am so glad to see you again.'

But who was that, also, on her knees, insisting on having his hand to cover it with kisses, sobbing and laughing, with tears and joy in eyes and voice? 'Oh, rallaluley. The maister be come back from that whist place!' Yes —Joyce. The true, devoted Joyce, who had only stayed an hour at Coombow with Mrs. Facey, and then had walked on, all night, and had come in—nay, burst in, on the Battishills in the morning, with the tidings that the master was on his way back to West Wyke. Over the chimney-piece, about the pictures, wherever it could be stuck, was bright holly with red berries. And see! hanging from the black beam, a bunch of mistletoe.

Herring's heart was full. He could not speak, but he took Cicely's head between his hands and kissed her; he stooped and lifted Joyce and pressed his lips to her cheek; and the old Squire's arm encircled him, and drew the young head down beside the old grey one.

The tongues of all failed. Herring raised his eyes, over which a mist was forming, and saw above the doorway an inscription in red holly berries—

Welcome Home.

By degrees only did the flush and fever of joy in these good simple souls subside, and Herring was able to recover his composure.

Then the young man stood by the Squire's chair and looked at him. His heart reproached him for having deserted him for so long a time.

'We hoped you would have dropped in and eaten your Christmas dinner with us, John,' said Mr. Battishill. 'We set your chair at the table, and a sprig of holly by your plate, in hopes you would arrive.'

'I am very sorry, sir, that I was not here. I should have been far happier here among such dear, kind friends.'

'It is you, John, who have been a kind friend to us,' said the old man. 'Just consider. If you had not rescued the mortgages out of Tramplara's hands when you did, they would have fallen to the creditors, the directors of Ophir, and we should have been turned into the cold.'

'You repay what little I have done for you a thousand fold,' answered Herring.

There was a flush on the old man's cheek, caused by excitement.

'Now we have you here again,' he said, 'you must remain with us, at all events, for some time. Consider this as your home.'

'Yes,' answered Herring, 'I have no home elsewhere.' He spoke sadly. Cicely looked hard at him. He went on, 'I will stay on with you till I tire you out with my society.'

'That can never be. There is Upaver crying out for you; I am past attending to that. I am not what I was a few months ago. The wheels are becoming rusty and the gear breaks.'

Cicely looked from her father to Herring questioningly. Did John note the change in the old man? A change there was; he was failing in many ways. Just now the delight of seeing Herring again had revived him, nevertheless the change was observable enough. The eager look had gone out of the eyes, and the lips had become more tremulous than ever.

As Cicely turned her eyes from one to the other, there dawned on her the truth that a change had come over John Herring—a change greater than that which had passed upon her father. She had not been apprised of this by Joyce, and was unprepared for it. She noticed it first with incredulity, then with perplexity, and she resolved to speak with him on the subject. The man was not the same. The same in outward feature, in colour of hair and eyes, but he was not the same in expression. He was aged. A wave had passed over his head, and he had come forth half drowned. The elasticity was gone from his tread, the sparkle from his eye, the dimple from his cheek, the laugh from his lips. The eye had become more steady, lines had formed on his brow and in his cheeks; the lips had lost their flexibility, they were closed and firm. He no longer held his head erect with strong self-consciousness; he seemed to have acquired a slight stoop, the head was somewhat bowed.

It was clear to Cicely that Herring had undergone some grievous trial, of what sort she could not guess, and that he had emerged from it with a strengthened character, though with a saddened heart. Cicely did not indeed take this in all at once. Her curiosity was roused and her attention fixed, and by degrees the greatness and significance of the change forced themselves upon her.

The old man observed nothing. But now Joyce, who had been thrust into the background, insisted on asserting herself.

'See, dear maister, what be come to your Joyce. Do'y look here!'

She stood forward in the light—the light of several candles, lit to welcome Herring home. She wore a dark-blue serge gown, and a white kerchief round her neck, and crossed over her bosom. Her luxuriant dark hair was combed and pruned, and fastened up under a white cap. The gown was short, and showed white stockings and black shoes. Her wild face was subdued and softened, the rudeness had gone out of it, and a strange tinge of sweetness and modesty had come in place of the savagery. She was really a handsome girl, of splendid physique, easy in every motion.

'Did'y ever see wonder like this?' asked Joyce, holding out her skirts and apron, and showing her white stockings. 'And see how grand my hair be. What do'y say to this, maister dear?'

'Why, Joyce, I congratulate you with all my heart. This is what I have been wishing for, but never hoped to see.'

'You have wished for it—you! O glory and blazes! I be glad.'

'I told you as much, Joyce,' said Cicely Battishill.

'I know you did, miss, but I couldn't believe it. I thought you sed it just to persuade me on.'

'Cousin John, we have enlarged our household to-day. We have taken Joyce in. Her dread of going under the "hellens" has given way. She will learn to make herself useful. Now, Joyce, you may go back to the kitchen, and help Charity to get supper ready.'

'What has become of the old man—Grizzly?'

'We allow him to sleep in one of the linneys, and he is given broken meat once a day. He has fallen into bad ways of late. Ophir injured him as much as it injured his superiors, only in a different way. He learned from the workmen to drink, and now he loafs about the country trying to get something given him by inconsiderate persons to keep his throat wet. He is at Upaver a good deal; there the miners make game of him, and treat him. He has taken to smoking. I have threatened that if he carries his pipe into the shippon, I shall refuse him the linney as a bedroom, and he will have to return to the Giant's Table.'

'I am glad that he and his daughter are parted.'

'There was no chance for her as long as she remained under his thraldom. Fortunately she had set her head on going for two months to a place called Coombow, and that opened the way to her leaving Grizzly altogether. He is a hopeless savage. We did believe at one time that he was capable of improvement. He worked hard on his patch of land. But Ophir diverted him from the upward path, and since then he has been going down hill nearly as fast as his barrel when it broke from its tether.'

'Well, John,' said Mr. Battishill, 'I must not let Cicely engross you. Come and talk to me. I will tell you what we have been doing at Upaver. We have got the leat cut, and the wheel and crushers in place, and a smelting house run up. I have not been able to go there myself, but the foreman, a very worthy, sensible fellow, comes up every other day and reports progress. I have seen to the accounts as you desired; but I am not what I was. My head has become confused, and I have had to ask Cicely to help me out with the accounts. I hope you will not find them in a great muddle, but I was never very precise, and ladies do not understand the difference between debit and credit sides of a balance sheet. The table of work is left with me, and I pretend to look it over, but have not the means of verifying it. I do not think much has come out of the mine yet. I cannot say the profits are large. Indeed, the credit side of the book is blank.'

'I do not expect anything yet. I am content that the machinery should be in place and in working order. Now I am here, we will attack the lode.'

'There is the rub, John; the machinery is up, but not in working order, the leat is cut, but the water won't run along it.'

'That will soon be rectified, and then the profits will come in freely.'

'I hope so, John.'

'I am sure of it, sir. Do not you lose heart.'

'I have made such a failure of life, John, that I have ceased to be sanguine. I can see nothing in the retrospect but blunders and losses.'

'No, sir, you have made mistakes, but all must do that before reaching success. Upaver was your own discovery.'

'That is true, very true. I think we will christen this mine Wheal Battishill.'

'Do you not think Wheal Cicely would sound better?' asked John Herring.

'My suggestion is the best,' said Cicely, colouring. 'Let it be Wheal Friendship.'

A bright and cosy supper. The great fireplace full of crackling flame. A white cloth on the black oak table near the fire, and silver and glass upon it sparkling in the candlelight, and the flicker of the flames embracing a huge faggot.

'Good luck never comes alone,' said the Squire. 'What do you think! My dear old friend, John Northmore, has sent me a couple of pheasants. I have not seen him for many years, and I do not know how he comes to remember me now; however that may be, he has, and most opportunely. Here comes one of his pheasants to table. I thought I was forgotten of all the world, but—I hope it is an omen of coming success to Wheal Friendship—old friends are beginning to remember that there is such a man as Richard Battishill, J.P.'

'Shall we sit down?' asked Cicely. 'Everything is ready.'

'Although my cates be poor, take it in good part,

Better cheer may you have, but not with better heart,'

quoted the Squire. 'You are godfather to the wine, John. It is some of the case you ordered down from Exeter. We will drink in it success to Wheal Friendship.'

The old man was garrulous and cheerful during supper. The family plate was brought out in honour of John Herring, and the Spode china, red with

57

burnished gold in leaf and scroll. How bright and comfortable the table was, how warm and cheery the room! What kindly happy faces were round the table! This was something like home.

The pain did not leave John Herring's heart, the cloud did not remove from his brain, but, under the influences now brought to bear upon him, the pain lost its first poignancy, and the cloud hung less deep. At the conclusion of supper, Cicely persuaded her father to go to bed. The old man was obstinate at first. 'He liked to be with John, and to chat with him over the fire. He had just begun to enjoy his wine. The room had only now become warm— why should he be banished to his cold chamber upstairs? He had not seen John for months, he had business to discuss with him. There was a good story he remembered, which he wished to tell him;' and so on, a string of reasons why he should not go to bed. But he was weak, and, though he was obstinate for a few minutes, yielded to his daughter's perseverance, and she helped him upstairs. John Herring remained by the fire. He was glad to be alone; he stood with his back to the fire, thinking. Two nights ago—forty-eight hours only— had passed since he had gone home to Welltown with his bride. Home!—was that home? The house half buried in snow was cold within, the reception was cheerless, no fire, no table spread, and, worst of all, no love from her whom he had taken to be his wife. He had been driven from that home with despair in his heart. He returned to West Wyke: the sun was shining, the birds singing, the flowers opening, the house was decked to receive him, and the kind hearts therein bounded to meet him.

Which was his real home? He raised his eyes to the door as it opened to readmit Cicely Battishill, and read over it, in scarlet letters, 'Welcome home!'

Cicely seated herself opposite him in the ingle nook, and the soft firelight played over her pleasant face and glowing auburn hair. She was a thrifty body, and she had put out all the candles save two on the great table. These were not really needed—the firelight filled the room.

'How do you think my father is looking?' she asked.

'He is greatly altered. I fear that his anxiety about both Ophir and Upaver has been too much for him.'

'Ophir did upset him greatly, but Upaver—Wheal Friendship, I mean—has done him good; it has occupied him, and taken his thoughts from his own infirmities. He thinks he is deep in business, and that amuses him. He schemes all sorts of things and suggests them to the foreman, who is too civil to say that they are impracticable. No, Upaver has been to him not a care but a distraction. That which ails him is general failure of power. The doctor has visited him and is very kind, and he can do nothing. The new parson at Tawton, Mr. Harmless Simpleton, has also called, and seen my father. He is a very admirable and agreeable gentleman.'

'Your father seemed cheerful this evening.'

'Yes, he was excited by your return. It has given him the greatest pleasure to see you here again. You do not know how he clings to you. Cousin John, I cannot express myself as I ought, but I feel very deeply thankful to you for having relieved and brightened the closing days of my father's life. We were threatened with disaster, and it seemed at one time as if he would sink, and utter ruin would cover and blot us both out. You have saved us, and now the dear old man's evening is like one which succeeds a day of cloud, when suddenly all the vapours roll away, and a blaze of golden sun glorifies the landscape. I believe that my father is as happy as he possibly can be now that he has you here.'

Herring made some commonplace remark in reply.

'Yes, we owe a great deal to you—more than we can ever repay,' said Cicely.

'You are going to make my fortune at Upaver,' said he, half jestingly.

'Oh, John! that is nothing to you. You do not care about that.' She paused for a couple of minutes, with her eyes on the fire, rocking her foot, her hands clasped over her knee. Presently she turned towards him, with sympathy in her honest eyes and in her trembling mouth. 'Do not be offended if I tell you what I have observed. There is a great change in you. I am sure you have gone through a time of great trouble. We were selfish, and vexed, and impatient, because you did not come to us. We thought you were amusing yourself elsewhere, and had forgotten us, and how much we depended on you. We had no suspicion that you were unhappy. I can see that you have had your cup of bitterness. Neither my father nor I have asked you any questions about yourself at any time, and we really know nothing about yourself and your belongings. I do not want to know anything now that you do not wish to tell me. Indeed, indeed, I would do or say my best to comfort you, if I thought that I were capable of making you happier by my interference. There was something you said just now to my father—it was only one sentence, but I saw that it contained in it the kernel of much trouble. My father bade you look on this house as your home. Then you answered that this was the only home you had. Did you really mean what you said?'

'Yes, Cicely. I have no home anywhere, except this that you offer me.'

'You have lost Welltown?'

He hesitated. Then he said in a low tone, 'I have lost it in one sense. It has ceased to be a home to me; the acres remain—that is all.'

'Oh, John, I am so sorry for you. I know you loved the place. I know what an ache it would give me to lose West Wyke.' She did not in the least understand what his loss really was. He did not enlighten her—indeed, it was not possible for him to do so.

Presently she returned to the charge.

'Have you any brothers or sisters?'

'None.'

'And your father and mother are dead?'

'Yes. My mother died when I was born, and I was reared by a nurse. I know her only by her picture.'

'John, tell me,' she looked at him very earnestly, and with her expressive

60

and sweet face full of compassion; 'tell me—have you no one then to love you?'

He shook his head. 'No one.'

'At Welltown—no one?'

'My nurse. No one else.'

'How lonely in the world you must be!'

'Utterly,' he answered.

Then she brightened up, and, dashing some tears from her eyes, held out her hands to him laughingly across the glowing hearth. 'There, there, poor boy! We have been talking of Cornwall. There you may be alone and unloved, but here, in old Devon, under the shadow of Cosdon, you have a home, and hearts that care a great deal for you; there is my father, here am I, then there is Joyce, and lastly my white cat! See! he is up on your knee this moment. There! never again say that you are solitary and unloved. It is not true, it is utterly false. Good-night, Cousin John! sweet sleep, happy dreams, and a glad awaking to you!'

CHAPTER XLVIII.

TWO BEQUESTS.

Next morning John Herring went early to Upaver. The wheel was up, and the leat had been cut. But the wall supporting the axle of the wheel was improperly built, and the leat was improperly levelled. Much that the contractor had undertaken to do had been left undone, and most that he had done was done so badly that it had to be done over again.

Herring called for the day-books, and soon saw that the men working for day wage had taken three days to do what might have been done in one, and that was work which need not have been done at all.

Ophir had demoralised the entire neighbourhood. The object aimed at there had been to make a great display of activity, but to produce nothing. What had been begun at Ophir, the workmen supposed was to continue at Upaver.

Herring rang the bell of the mine, and called the men together. He dismissed the foreman on the spot—that civil and intelligent foreman whom Mr. Battishill esteemed so highly. He told the men that henceforth he would be their captain; he would be at Upaver every day, and would set every man his work, and what he set each man he expected him to execute. A fair day's work for a fair wage, and no payment for idle hours. Those who disliked his terms might go elsewhere in quest of new Ophirs. There was one subsidiary matter he wished to speak of. Old Grizzly Cobbledick was much at the mine, and was treated by the men. He disapproved of this. He would not have the old man given drink and made sport of there. If he would work, he should be given work; if he were determined to get drunk, he must get his drink elsewhere.

Then Herring examined the adit.

Much the same story there as outside. The work had been gone on with anyhow, the ore thrown out with the cable.

He did not return to West Wyke to dinner in the middle of the day; he was too busy. He remained in the mine, and made the men dig whilst he was present. The vein 'bunched,' and the bunch of nearly pure metal was before him. A rich profit was a certainty.

When the men knocked off work, he turned to go to West Wyke. He was covered with dirt, but he was in good spirits. He had not been mistaken. Upaver mine would clear the property of its incumbrances, and repay every penny that had been sunk in it. Mirelle's money had been invested in the mortgages, Mirelle's money had been spent on the mine. Her money was not only safe, it was where it would yield excellent interest.

As Herring came away, he found Grizzly awaiting the men leaving work, to beg of them tobacco, a draught of cyder or spirits, or some coppers.

'I want to speak to you,' said Herring. 'Come along with me.'

Grizzly trudged at his side. There had been a rude savagery in the man when Herring had first known him which was not without its dignity. Old Cobbledick had then worked on his own land, grown his own potatoes, lived in his own house, and thrashed his own child. The consciousness of independence had given him an upright carriage and an open and haughty look. All this was gone. Ophir had robbed him of the one redeeming element in his nature. He had found it easier to beg than to work. He had abandoned all attempt at labour for a livelihood, and with that had lost independence. Formerly he had been defiant in his sense of freedom, he was now cringing in his submission. He had been a temperate man, drinking only water; now he drank whenever he could find any one to treat him, and whatever was given to him. Association with men higher than himself in civilisation had lowered, not lifted, him. It is so with all savages when brought in contact with civilisation; some seize the moment, and mount, others are cast into deeper degradation than they knew before. It is so with ourselves when set within the orbit of higher and nobler forces than we knew before. They exercise on us a centripetal or a centrifugal energy. Cobbledick was debased. His rags of old had become him, they now made him repulsive; he had ceased to be a man, and had become a scarecrow.

'I want to speak to you, Cobbledick,' said Herring, walking on his way, the old man at his side.

'Your honour! I be all ears. It be the backie sure-ly has a come into your head.'

'It is the drink, Grizzly; the drink.'

'Oh!' exclaimed Cobbledick, 'to think I lived these scores and scores of years without a knowing what it were. But now—glory rallaluley! Praises be!

I can get drunk when I meets a real gemman.'

'Grizzly, I have forbidden the men at the mine to give you anything. If you choose to come there and work, I will find you work that you can do, but if I discover that the men give you drink, and encourage you in your idle, vagabond ways, I shall dismiss them, and find others who will obey me. Mark this, Grizzly, not another drop of anything, in treat or otherwise, do you get at Upaver. Go back to the Giant's Table, and dig your fields there like a man, instead of slouching about, picking up halfpence and sips of gin, a wretched beggar.'

'I ain't to get nothing to Upaver?' asked Cobbledick, incredulously.

'Do you not understand plain words? Not a drop. I will not have Upaver a curse to you and others, such as Ophir was. If you will work, I will give you tasks equal to your powers.'

'Ekal to my powers!' roared Grizzly; 'look at my hands. See, they be two, three times as big as yours. I could break every bone in your body with mun. I be strong; I reckon, stronger than most of they fellows down to Upaver.'

'Very well, then, work.'

'I won't work. I ain't forced.'

'No, I am sorry for it. It is a mistake that you are given broken scraps from West Wyke. That keeps you from famishing, and emancipates you from the necessity of working.'

'You'd cut me off that next, I reckon.'

'Yes, I would.'

'You would!' repeated the old man malevolently. 'You takes away my liquor, and my meat, and my daughter as ought to work and keep me in my old age, and'—he turned and looked up in Herring's face—'you took the box from under the hearthstone.'

Herring started. The old man observed his advantage and chuckled.

'Grizzly, it is quite true that I took the box. You had no right to it; you had stolen it from the carriage that was upset. I took it that I might return it _____,'

'Oh, in coorse, in coorse, you returned the box at once, and all that was in it, to the young lady with the white face.'

Herring could not answer. The old man, with his natural shrewdness, saw that he had gained an advantage. Of the value of the contents of the box he had no idea. He determined to improve his advantage.

'You took thicky box, as you take to plundering me of everything I has. I reckon you'd like to take from me the chance of sleeping in the linney.'

'Yes, I would, Grizzly. Whatever I deprive you of is for your own advantage. It is not safe for you to lie in the straw of the linney. I know that you have gone in there more than once, tipsy, and smoking your pipe.'

'Well, what then?'

'Why, you may be setting fire to the linney, and burn that and the house, and yourself as well. However, to return to the box. If that box had been found in your possession by any one but myself, you would have been sent to prison. The box was not yours. It was stolen. If I desire now to deprive you of drink, it is because drink is degrading you. I want to force you to work.'

'I won't work no more,' said Cobbledick, angrily. 'There be the backie, also. You've never paid me that.'

'What tobacco?'

'Ah! when you was sick, and my Joyce nussed you under the Table, you got in debt to me a score pounds and one more, that be as many as you've a got fingers and toes, and your head throwed in to make another. That be what you've owed me a long while, and never paid yet. There were that old Tramplara, he owed me scores and scores of backie, but he never paid me none at all. He went scatt. I did think you were a gemman, and would serve a poor man better.'

'I do not understand about the tobacco.'

'Loramussy! it be easy enough to understand, sure-ly. You was brought here in a waggon; well, that waggon had to be paid for, and my Joyce paid with her work, and then she was a neglecting of me. You were brought to my house, and I had to clear out and go elsewhere, and after that Joyce did nothing more for me. You expect me and my Joyce to work for'y, and you never pay a brass farthing? No gemman be like that. I call that a proper blaggard trick, I do.'

'Good heavens, Grizzly! If you want to be paid for the use of your house because it served as my hospital, by all means name the price. I will pay you in tobacco if you desire it. How much do you require?'

'As many pounds as you've fingers and toes, and your head chucked in.'

'You shall have them.'

'And then,' pursued Grizzly, 'there be Joyce. What hev you gone and tooked 'er away from me for? Oh! ah! you've not? That be fine. Her worked peaceable enough for her poor old vaither till you come by and turn 'er head with your talking and sweethearting——'

'Grizzly!' exclaimed Herring, angrily, 'hold that villanous tongue of yours at once.'

'Ah, you don't want to be told of all the wrongs you've a done to me. Oh dear! the deal of pains and expense as her hev a put me to, what with her rearing, and her feeding, and her clothing, and—that is to be all for nort. When her be good full growed and able-bodied, and might work for her old vaither, then you draws 'er away for reasons of your own, and leaves me without a child. Now her can't think of me, nor work for me, nor light a fire for me, nor cook a biling of turnips, nor wire a rabbit—all becos you've a turned her head so as her can think, and talk, and work only for the young maister, and I'm to bide content with a score and one of backie. That ain't in reason. That ain't how a gemman would act. Why, there were a man t'other day to Okehampton market brought his wife there with a halter round her neck and sold 'er there for half a crown—not for backie, but for a real half-crown in silver.[1] Her were oldish, and not like my Joyce. If I be to part wi' Joyce, I'll take nort but silver for her, and I won't be content wi' less nor four half-crowns. I've got to make my own fire now, and do everything myself. Not you, nor Miss Cicely, nor the old Squire shall stay me. I won't sell 'er not a penny under four half-crowns and some'ut over to wet the bargain with. If you don't accept my terms I'll have her back, and if her sez her won't come back I'll do by her as I did afore—I'll just scatt all the bones she has to her body. Her got her bones o' me, and I've a right to do what I will wi' my own. I can scatt mun or I can sell mun. And I won't sell mun a penny under five half-crowns, that be my figure, and blast me blue if I takes a shilling off. I'd rather break her bones first and dung my pertaty ground wi' 'em. Feel my hands, how strong they be.'

[1] The author knew the woman thus purchased, and the man who bought her, and with whom she lived till her death. The transaction took place about forty years ago, as described.

He suddenly laid hold of Herring's wrists, and his grasp was as an iron vice. Herring was a strong man, but he was unprepared to meet and resist such strength as the old savage exhibited.

'Did her give you the shining stones in the box? I reckon it were so, and her knows what to expeck for doing that, and I'll do it. Did I go and take the box from the carriage? And can the constable come and carry me off to gaol for that? Then surely, if I say to un, there be the young Squire to West Wyke have a been to the Giant's Table and have a took away my daughter, then if there be justice for one there be justice for another, and the constable will come and carry you to gaol also.'

Herring walked on quicker. He was alarmed for Joyce. It would be wrong to send her back to her father. She had risen to a higher level than he; she could not associate with him longer. Moreover, he was uneasy at his threats, for the wretched old man, as he knew, would execute them without compunction.

'Six half-crowns I sed, and if you won't buy her of me for yourself, and give me the money in silver, I'll fetch her home to the Table, and I'll scatt every bone in her body, I will, glory rallaluley! You ain't a going to take everything from me, and give nothing in return.'

'There!' exclaimed Herring, angrily; 'take that.' He drew his purse from his pocket, and dashed it at the old man. It struck him on the chest, and Grizzly had his hand on it in a moment.

'I can catch,' said he. 'The men chucks me bits of their pasties, and I can snap like a dog. I never lets mun drop.'

'Take that and torment Joyce no more. You will find ample in that purse to supply you with tobacco, and drink too, if you will have it. Take it, you despicable scoundrel, and leave the poor girl alone.'

'A sale be a sale,' said Grizzly. 'If you've a bought her, you have her and I've nort more to say to her. I sed seven half-crowns. Dash my brains out if I sed a penny less.' Cobbledick opened the purse and peeped in. 'Oh, rallaluley! them be guineas! golden guineas! they be worth more than eight half-crowns, the price I axed for Joyce, I reckon. Shan't I only smoke backie and get drunk. Glory! glory!'

'Do as you will. Some men cannot be helped. One must let them go to the devil their own way. You are one, and the sooner you go the better.'

'I be going. I be going as fast as I can,' exclaimed the old man, misunderstanding him.

'Then go, and do not trouble Joyce any more.'

'Oh no. I've a sold her to you. Don't'y come and try to cry off the bargain, and want your guineas back. This be scores better deal than that of the man with his wife in Okehampton market. Now, what about the linney?'

'You may not sleep there, not on any account, if you are bent on getting drunk and smoking. I'll send you down some straw with which to litter the Giant's Table.'

'Oh, rallaluley! this be fine games.' And the old savage dashed off over the moor.

Thus ended Herring's attempt at reformation of Grizzly Cobbledick. He had gone forth that morning resolved to check the old man in his downward career by cutting off the occasion of drinking, and he had supplied the man with the means of drinking himself to death.

However, he went his way, relieved in mind, to West Wyke. He had saved Joyce from further unpleasantness from her father.

Cicely met him in the porch.

'You have been a long time out,' she said. 'My father has been calling for you all day. He is very feeble; you will notice how different he is from what you saw him last night. The excitement of your return stimulated him, and now has come the relapse. Hark! I hear him calling.'

Herring went in, with her.

'Papa has only come down this afternoon. I persuaded him to lie in bed during the morning, but when he thought you would be returning from Upaver he insisted on being dressed and descending to meet you.'

'John, is that you?' called the old Squire from his chair by the fire.

'Yes, sir. I have been all day at Upaver. I have got news to tell you. We have come on a bunch of metal which I hope will clear you of all care.'

Mr. Battishill nodded. 'Yes, yes!'

The news did not seem to interest him greatly. Herring saw with concern that he was looking feeble and old. He had fallen back sadly after the flicker of last night.

'I am not strong,' said the Squire; 'I cannot speak loud or long to-day. Come here.' He took John Herring by the hand. 'Come, Sissy.' He beckoned Cicely to draw near. 'John, I fear my time is coming to an end. I have been trying to-day to become interested in Upaver, but I cannot. I can only fix my mind on one thing. Perhaps when that is settled, then I may be able to hear about Upaver, but not till then.'

'Do not lose heart, Mr. Battishill, now that you are on the threshold of success.'

'It is this, John. Should I have another stroke, or be unable to attend to matters, what is to become of Cicely? What is to become of West Wyke? I want your promise that you will stand by her and the old place.'

'I will do all I can for her, and for West Wyke. You may rely on me, sir.'

'I felt convinced in my own mind that I might do so, and yet I desired your promise. I became troubled, and clouds came over my spirits. As Sebastian says, "My determinate voyage is mere extravagancy." It always has been so with me. I have set my mind on the wrong things, and gone the wrong ways to work when I took anything in hand. But it is not so now. Owls can see in the dark, and so can I. If I have made blunders hitherto, I will hit straight this time. I have your promise, have I not, John?'

'Yes, Mr. Battishill.'

'You will not desert poor Sissy. She has no relations, and I have positively no one in the world to look to except yourself, whom, upon my word, I have come to love and regard as a son.' The old man patted Herring affectionately on the shoulder.

'I give you my promise, sir.'

'There! that makes me content,' said the old man. He had taken Cicely's hand in his left, he held John by the right. All at once he put their hands together. 'There!' he said, and chuckled, 'as Hamlet says, "There is a kind of confession in your looks, which your modesties have not craft enough to colour." I know you love each other. I give Cicely to you, John, and my blessing. You will take care of her—and, you will quarter the owls.'

He leaned back and his eyes closed. He was satisfied that at last he had done the right thing at the right time. The fatal faculty of making muddle and mischief followed him to the end.

Herring turned to Cicely and released his hand. She was trembling.

'You, Cicely, insisted that we were cousins. You have heard your father: he has made the relationship closer. We are henceforth brother and sister.'

She looked up, then her eyes fell, and the colour rose and sank in her face.

'Yes,' she said faintly; 'I understand perfectly, *brother John*.'

CHAPTER XLIX.

CAST UP.

'It be good for the soul to see men die,' said Genefer, entering Mirelle's room. 'Come along of me, mistress.'

'What is it, Genefer? Do not frighten me.'

'In the midst of life we are in death. It teaches us how frail and uncertain our life be. Come and see 'em die afore your naked eyes.'

'Genefer, I will not!' Mirelle held back in alarm.

'You must come. The wreck is drifted right into Welltown cove, and it will be your own rocks as will break the ribs of the vessel and cut the flesh off the bones of the drownded. If there be a chance to save any of the poor creatures on board of her, then you must be there to direct what is to be done. You be mistress here now. I know my duty; so do Hender. When the master weren't here, and afore you comed, it were different. But now, it be not Hender nor me as be answerable. It be you as is put in authority, and have to say to this man, Come, and he cometh, and to another, Go, and he goeth. If you bide at home and do nothing, then let 'em be drownded, and them as has done good shall enter into life, and them as has done evil shall go into everlasting death, and the blood of the souls that be lost shall rest on your head.'

'But what is it?'

'I tell you there be a vessel drove by the storm right in, and her be drifting into Welltown cove. It be no good her trying to get into Boscastle Harbour, with the white horses galloping. Her comes side on upon the reef, and will go scatt afore your eyes.'

'Can nothing be done?'

'You must be there and see,' answered Genefer Benoke: 'if there be lives to be saved, they will be saved, but you must be there to see to it.'

Mirelle put on her cloak and hat, and went forth. This was a duty, and Mirelle had a strong sense of obligation to do her duty, whenever it was presented before her.

The storm of last night had subsided, and the wind had shifted. A thaw had set in, and the sun was streaming over the melting snow. The blue sea was strewn with foam streaks. Though the wind had abated, the sea was still churning. The passion of the night could not abate at once; the pulses of the Atlantic were throbbing. The sight was magnificent. The billows that rolled upon the headland were at once shattered, and sent up columns of foam white as the snow upon the ground. Earlier, the morning sun had painted rainbows in the salt drift, but now the sun hung over the sea, and, if he painted them still, did so unseen by those on land. The whole coast was fringed with a deep border of fluttering white lace. The air was salt, and the lips of all who faced it became briny. Out at sea stood the Meachard, an islet of inaccessible black rock, capped with turf. On this no snow rested. The waves besieged the Meachard on all sides, like the rabble of Paris attacking the Bastille; they appeared to explode on touching the rock into volumes of white steam, that rushed up, whirling, and swept the crown. The reflection of the sun in the sea was shivered into countless, ever-changing flakes of fire. Over the surface of the water the gulls were fluttering in vast numbers—they seemed like sea foam vivified.

This was the sea after the storm, already exhausted, and with relaxed power. What must it have been in the height of its rage, during the night?

'Where is the ship?' asked Mirelle, looking in vain for a vessel on the uneasy surface.

'Look!' old Genefer pointed.

'What, that? It is so small.'

'There be men aboard, living and calling on God now, and in ten minutes they'll be standing afore their Judge. They can look out of their eyes now, and see you up here on the cliff in your black gown, and in ten minutes their eyes will be full of salt water, and able to see nothing. They can cry aloud for mercy now, and in ten minutes the time of mercy will be over for each, and the time of retribution will be begun!'

Mirelle could hardly believe that the little cockleshell drifting on the rocks before her could contain men in jeopardy of their lives. It was but a cockleshell, a child's ship made of a walnut. But there were men and women on the headland watching intently and with interest the fate of that petty boat, and an excise officer stood there with his telescope to his eye.

'She is the "Susanna" of Bristol,' said he.

'Her's never been in our harbour,' observed a Boscastle man. 'I reckon there be about four aboard. Her be about the size to carry four.'

'What be the lading, Pentecost?'

'That don't matter to you or I, Gerans,' answered Pentecost. 'Times be altered when an honest man might profit by what the Lord sent us.'

'It do seem a deadly shame that a man may not accept the good gifts Providence showers upon him, but the Government must interfere.'

'Ah!' put in Genefer, 'that be the way of things. The sower sows his seed, and the fowls come and carry it away. The Lord sows His word, and the Church passons come and take it away that it can bring forth no fruit, and leave nort in its place. It is the same when He sends a storm and casts a ship ashore. A Christian man may not stoop and take up a keg of brandy the Lord has rolled to his feet, but the 'xisemen must come and take it away, so to speak, out of his mouth.'

'There be five shillings for every corpse as be picked up and brought to burial,' said another. 'But I'd rather have a keg of spirits than a corpse any day. Besides, who's to earn a crown like that? They may do it on the shores of Essex that be mud and sand. But here! old Uncle Zacky goes about after a storm with a sack, and picks up what gobbets of human flesh he can find on the shore, but the parish won't give un more than half a crown for as much as he can carry up the cliffs, and that takes a sight more picking up than would a whole corpse. These bain't times in which honest men may live.'

'I say, maister!' called Pentecost to the preventive man; 'spose her be laiden with sea coal, and the coal come ashore. Do'y put your foot down on that and say nobody ain't to shovel that up, it belongs to his Majesty, God bless him? And next tide the coal be all licked down into the belly of the ocean, and is no good to none.'

'What be the good of us keeping donkeys?' asked Gerans; 'I reckon they cost us something for hay in winter. Us don't keep donkeys for nort; us keep 'em to bring up the cliffs whatever comes ashore. And us is to have the expense of keeping donkeys and not to put 'em to no use! We are to keep the donkeys for the delight of our eyes, as beautiful objecks of nature.'

'I reckon her be laden with cloam' (earthenware) 'ovens,' said Pentecost. 'I wish his Majesty joy of them when they comes ashore. If Job were here and wanted a shard to scratch himself withal, and ventured to pick up a bit of scatted cloam off the beach, you'd be down on him in a jiffy, wouldn't you now, maister?'

The preventive officer took no notice of the gibes cast at him; he kept his telescope on the vessel.

'Her be on the breakers now,' said one of the men.

'What be the good of staying here?' asked another. 'There be no chance of getting nothing unless us was to chuck this chap over the cliffs first.'

'Don't say that, Pascho; there'll be five shillings for every corpse we can bring up the cliffs. And if we manage to save one alive, surely the young lady here will give us a trifle and a drop of cyder to drink her health and the corpse's. I seez it in her eye.'

'I will give you ten guineas for every man you save,' said Mirelle, vehemently, 'and as much as you can eat and drink.'

'Didn't I tell you so?' exclaimed Pentecost. 'Look alive, boys! There be the ship gone scatt! Down the cliffs with you all, and see if we cannot earn a few gold guineas and drink long life to the lady and the corpse as we brings up alive.'

The ship had struck. The waves and foam swept over her, and in a few moments she went to pieces. Some figures were discernible battling with the water. It seemed to Mirelle impossible that these tiny ants were sufferers, that they were of human flesh and feelings like herself—they seemed so small. There was nothing horrible in the sight: it was not so shocking as the drowning of mice turned out of a trap into a bucket. When Gulliver cried with pain in Brobdingnag, the giants laughed. In a microscopic creature the agony of death must be microscopically small.

Mirelle looked on the drowning pigmies, quite unable to realise the awfulness of the event, her sympathy stirred by her reason, not by her heart, for the appeal was not such as could move the sympathy save through the brain.

The first to sink was the mate. We will fly over the water with the gulls, instead of straining our eyes from the cliffs. Are the gulls about us screaming or laughing? The first to sink was the mate. He was an old seaman, a godfearing man, honest of heart, who had left the sea because he had earned enough to maintain himself on land in his old age. But he had lent his money to a younger brother, to enable him to set up a small shop in Bristol. The brother failed and ran away, leaving a wife and four little children wholly unprovided for. So the old man went to sea again to earn enough to support his brother's deserted wife and children. He sank. The gulls are cynics—they laughed.

The second that sank was the captain; a fine man, upright, rough in exterior, but soft-hearted. He had been an unlucky man. Engaged to a girl he had long loved, after many years of waiting, in which both turned the corner of life, he was now making his last voyage before he married her. She was at Bristol, preparing the little house they had taken. She had put flower-pots in the window, and was this morning setting a geranium there, to make the place look bright for the return of William and her own marriage. Then he sank. She would not see him again. The gulls laughed.

The third who sank was a boy, the only son of a widow. The boy had wanted much to go to sea, but he was the darling of his mother, and she would not suffer him to go with any but our captain, whom she knew and could trust with the only being on earth she loved. Now he was gone, and the widow must weep. The gulls laughed.

The fourth who went down was a sailor, a careless fellow, drinking and heeding neither angel nor devil; but there was a vein of gold in his heart waiting to be brought to the surface. It is said that on midsummer night all buried treasures rise and shine. Midsummer night had not come to him yet. Another year, and he would be a better man, but this other year was denied him. He sank, and the gulls laughed.

These were all who sank, but there was one who came ashore. He and the boy were clinging to the same piece of timber. Then this man kicked the boy on the chest and so he fell off and went down, and this man had the balk to himself. The waves went over him, and he lost consciousness, but not his hold. He was saved, and the gulls, wheeling above, laughed and scoffed more loudly than before.

Up the narrow track cut in the face of the cliff this man was carried.

'By goll!' said Pascho, 'I hope the chap ain't dead, but he looks cruel bad. It makes all the difference to us between five shillings and ten guineas.'

'Now look here, you niggers!' exclaimed Pentecost, angrily. 'What be all you a coming up and making believe you are helping? You've had nort to do with the saving of this chap, and so don't you come putting in your claims for a share. Go back and see if you can't pick up a corpse or two as will find you in liquor or backie for a week or a fortnight. The ten guineas is to share between five of us? and that will be four too many. I lugged un out of the water.'

'Ah, but I squeedged the water out of his chest,' said Pascho.

'And if I hadn't held the rope,' said Gerans, 'you'd have all been swept into the water and become crowners' sittings.'

'There!' said Pentecost, 'chuck him across a barrel, and let the water run out of him.'

'There be no barrel here; lay him flat.'

'Yes, in the snow indeed. Do you think I want to risk my honest earnings that way? He must be took to bed and hot bricks be put to his feet.'

'Where is he to go to?' asked Pascho.

'To Welltown, of course; where else? There ain't no other house nigh.'

'Let the young lady see un,' said Genefer. 'It be a rare fine sight for the soul to see a man hanging atween life and death. Let her see un.'

The men laid their unconscious burden at the feet of Mirelle.

She looked into the face with mingled sympathy and terror. The figure seen battling with the waves had grown big—human size now, it was no longer an ant. She could feel pity.

As she looked, she started and shrank away, holding up her hands to shut out what she saw.

'There!' said Genefer, 'it be a brave and improving sight. I reckon it do as much good to the soul as a lump of sugar with a drop of peppermint on it does to the stomick when out of sorts. It warms and strengthens and gives tone. He be a young man. Well, the Lord, I reckon, has got a work in store for he, as He has called him out of the deep, and has given him the life back as were trembling at the door of his heart to leave. As for the rest, they be cut off in their sins. Take him to Welltown.'

'Stay, stay!' exclaimed Mirelle, interposing with vehemence. 'He shall not—he shall never go thither. Never, so long as I am mistress there.'

'Is he to lie here on the snow?' asked Genefer. 'You will have to give an account of it if he do, and die in consequence.'

'He shall not be taken to Welltown.'

The men looked at each other.

'Where be we to carry un to, then?' asked Pentecost.

'If he die, I'm danged if it be fair if you deny us the ten guineas. He has life in him now, and if he lose it, it will be your fault, young lady. We've done our parts and earned our money.'

'Take him where you will, but not to Welltown.'

'There is no other house near.'

'Here,' said Mirelle, her hand trembling: 'here is the key; take him into the slate-quarry office. There is a bed there.'

'Ay, let him go there,' said Genefer; 'he can be cared for there just as well as at Welltown.'

The men stooped and raised the unconscious man again. Mirelle covered her eyes—the man saved was Sampson Tramplara.

She had promised ten guineas—and that ten guineas had saved his worthless life. Well for her had she at this juncture offered fifty to have him tossed back into the sea. The men would not have done it for twenty—there were too many present; they would have hesitated for thirty. But for fifty, he would have troubled her no more.

CHAPTER L.

TWO DISOBEDIENCES.

Next day Orange arrived. Mirelle had sent for her; she could not remain longer alone at Welltown, especially now that young Sampson was so near. She did not go to the office on Willapark to see him; she did not inquire after him. But she told Genefer that he was to be supplied with whatever he needed, and was to remain where he was till he was well enough to leave, and then he was to go his way.

As soon as Orange arrived Mirelle told her that Sampson had been saved from drowning after shipwreck, and was at the office; and Orange went immediately to see him.

Sampson was now quite recovered from his submersion. The fire was lighted in the stove, and the room was warm.

'Oh! you have come, have you?' he asked, when Orange entered. 'Not wise, I reckon, unless you are bent on bringing observation on me. What is this I hear? I am on Herring's land and in his office! This is a queer state of affairs; but the wheel of fate in its revolutions lands one in strange places, and places where one would least like to be. How came you here?'

Orange explained to him what had taken place since his disappearance; how Mirelle had been married to John Herring, and she had been brought to Welltown.

'That's queer. I haven't seen either him or her.'

'I am told that he has been called away on business—military, I suppose —and you cannot be surprised if she has not chosen to see you. She knows well enough who you are. But now, Sampson, about yourself. How came you here? And—are you safe, quite safe, here?'

'No, I arn't, that's the cussedness of it all. I can't stay here, especially now the Countess Candlesticks knows of my presence and has got a tongue in her head. If I stay here I shall be taken, and I can't go, because I have no money to go with.'

'How came you here?'

'Cast up by the sea, I reckon,' answered Sampson.

'But how came you to be wrecked?' asked Orange.

'Why, because I was aboard ship.'

'You may as well answer me civilly,' said his sister. 'If you get away from this place, it will be by my help, and I must know all about you, and whither you want to go.'

'Curse it,' said Sampson, 'if you want to know whence I have come I will tell you—from Bristol, and if you want to know why I left, it is because Polly Skittles has blown on me. If you want to know where I am going, you must be content to remain in ignorance, for I don't know myself.'

'But, Sampson, how came you to be in Bristol?'

'Because it was not my intention to run to France, or any place where I could not speak a word of their damned parleyvous. I don't see why a fellow should not lie snug in England instead of going into exile abroad. So, when I had to leave Launceston, I cut off first to Plymouth; but there I became funky, that was too near home, and so I made for Bristol, and there I've been enjoying myself ever since, and might have been living at ease like a fighting cock but for Polly Skittles.'

'You behaved abominably, Sampy. You carried off all the money that was in the house, and left mother and me absolutely destitute.'

'Oh, ah! I was not such a fool as to leave anything. Every one for himself is my maxim. But be reasonable; if I had left money you would not have had it, the creditors would have been down on you and have carried off everything. By George! I have had many a laugh over that Ophir since I have washed my hands of it. That was a rare plant, better than Polpluggan. And father did come out splendid in it. The way in which he beat old Flamank's covers and bagged his game was superlative. Well, he died like Wolfe at

81

Quebec. "They run! Who run?" "The Ophirites." And didn't they run!'

Sampson clapped his knees and roared.

'It strikes me that it was you who ran,' said Orange, sullenly. 'Now, tell me, what are you going to do?'

'I'll tell you one thing I have learned, and I had to go to Bristol to learn it. Orange, never trust a woman. I might have been all right now but for Polly Skittles. I was an ass, I allow that. I sent word to her at the Pig and Whistle where I was, and asked her to come to me and share my fortune with me. Well, she couldn't keep her tongue in her head, but was bragging about the rich man she was going to marry, and so from hint to circumstance, and all was blown. The beaks were on the scent and after me, and I had to make a run for it. I got on board the "Susanna" for Port Isaac. I thought if I managed to get there, I might give them the slip again. And now, damn it all, here am I stranded at Boscastle, and when the news reaches Bristol that the "Susanna" has been lost, it will be known also that I am saved, and the beaks will be after me again.'

'What has become of the money, Sampson?'

'Oh, blast it! there is the mischief. I brought away all I had with me, and it has gone down in the "Susanna." I did have some trifle about me when I came ashore, but those who saved my life relieved me of my purse. That was natural, and I cannot complain; I'd have done the same. But I am mad to think that all the gold of Ophir lies at the bottom of the Atlantic.'

'What is to be done now?'

'You must provide me with money.'

'Nonsense, Sampy. I—I have nothing. You know that well enough.'

'I don't know anything about it. You're clever enough to get what you want. You hooked Captain Trecarrel fast enough when you had set your mind on having him.'

Orange became scarlet. 'You are cruel, Sampson; you are worse, you are

82

brutal. I will have nothing more to say to you.'

'Yes, you will,' said he, insolently. 'If you don't I'll go myself to Welltown, and force that pale-faced fool to give me money.'

'You know that she was plundered as well as others. Her money was sunk in Ophir.'

'I know that she can take her husband's money now. I suppose she has wit enough to keep the keys of his cash-box. Women are not such fools as to omit that.'

'I cannot ask her for money; indeed I cannot, Sampy.'

'Look here, Orange. How the devil am I to get away from this place without blunt? And how am I to live when I get away without ditto? You don't suppose I can dig and plough, do you?'

'I tell you I have nothing.'

'Then you must get me something. I've been overhauling this office and I can find nothing in it. There is a drawer locked in the desk that I have not opened and examined, but I shall know its contents before long, even if I have to break the lock. I don't, however, expect to get much out of it. A man does not leave money in such an uninhabited place as this.'

'If I get you a little you must be content with that.'

'If you get me a little I will be content with it only as long as it lasts, and when spent, then I shall want more.'

'What folly this is! You carried off every penny you could lay hands on, and now you ask for money from those you have plundered.'

'I do not ask you for your own money, I know you have none to give. I want some of Mirelle's money, or her husband's—it is all the same. Get me her diamonds if you can. Do you not understand? I dare not remain here above a day longer; I must be off before the beaks are on my track. How is a man to get away without a penny in his pocket? He must halt and beg on his road, and where he begs there he is observed. I must double on the hounds on their way hither. If I make for Bath I shall do. They are sure to run to Port Isaac, whither the "Susanna" was bound.'

'I wish you were safe away. I do not relish your being here. It would be exceedingly unpleasant for me were you taken whilst I am at Welltown. I do not want ugly stories to get about this neighbourhood, for here my mother and I will have to live.'

'I don't suppose you do,' answered Sampson; 'more the reason why I should be given facilities for clearing off.'

'I really do not know what to do. I might represent to Mirelle that you had lost everything, and ask her for a little money, a few pounds; but I cannot, I will not, entreat for a large sum.'

'Why not?'

'Because it is against my own interest. I am not yet settled into the house. I have but arrived to-day, and if my mother and I are to take up our quarters here, I must not begin by making myself disagreeable to the hostess. You know what Mirelle is. She is simple in some things, but when you think you are going to turn her round your fingers, you discover that she is the most impracticable person you ever had to deal with.'

'I say, Orange, what about those diamonds of hers?'

'They are paste.'

'I don't believe it.'

'She gave me part of the set, the pendant, and the stones in that were all artificial.'

'You fool,' said Sampson, 'that was why she gave you the brooch. If they had been real, do you suppose that she would have made you such a handsome present?'

'I do not know,' answered Orange, sullenly. She was angry with

Sampson, and she wanted to get rid of him. It would suit her very well to live with Mirelle. She hated Launceston, and wished to leave it. She trusted that something was going to be done for her by Mirelle in fulfilment of the promise made by John Herring on the wedding day, but she was not certain. At all events it was most convenient for her to live with Mirelle, and, if she were given money, to lay it by. She had indignantly rejected the suggestion of taking Captain Trecarrel, but she loved him still, and she entertained a lingering hope of future reconciliation. If he wanted her, he would come after her. She had sufficient sound sense to know that he could not marry her if she was without private means, because he was poor himself. She was jealous of Mirelle. The Captain had hovered about her; Mirelle had drawn him off from her. She was not at all sure that the Captain would desist from his attentions now that Mirelle was married. She wished, therefore, to be with her rival so as to watch her.

'Orange!'

'Well, Sampson.'

'I say. We were always allies.'

'To what does this introduction lead?'

'Where does Mirelle keep her diamonds?'

'I do not know. I have come here to-day for the first time.'

'I wish you would find out.'

'I can find out fast enough.'

'I say, Orange. If I could finger them, you wouldn't see much of me for many a day, and that is what your sisterly heart desires.'

'I wish I could be sure of that.'

'You are not over fond of the Countess Candlesticks, I reckon.'

'I hate her,' answered Orange, vehemently.

'You would not mind getting those diamonds for me, would you? She don't want them. What use can she make of them in a desert like this? She would not miss them.'

'I tell you, Sampy, I do not know where they are, and what is more, if I did know, I would not give them to you. I am not going to risk my place in the house for you.'

'Who is to see you take them? Lay the blame on me. Find out where they are and tell me, and if accessible I will work my way into the house and get them.'

'It won't do; it won't do indeed. If I knew where the stones were, I would not mind telling you; and if you could get them without risk of detection, and without in any way involving me, I would not care. But I will not help you to them.'

'If I had them, I'd be off to America at once.'

'There—I must go now,' said Orange, rising. 'I will try to get you something, but you must not expect much.' She turned to go out. She was flushed and annoyed. The presence of Sampson was vexatious to her, and might prove inconvenient.

'Stay a moment, Orange. Have you any keys about you?'

'I must go—yes, I have. I brought away the bunch from Dolbeare, in my haste. What will mother do without them?'

'She can send for the blacksmith, I cannot. Leave them with me. I want to look inside that drawer. There is a file in the cupboard, and I can make a key fit the lock I intend to open. Thank you, Orange. You are a good sister— worthy of me. You do credit to your father also. Now you may go.'

In the night a tap sounded at the door of Willapark office. Sampson had been working hard and was tired. He was snoozing in the chair over the fire. He started instantly to full consciousness and in alarm. His fears subsided when the door opened, and he saw Orange enter, very white and trembling.

'Well,' he said, 'what have you brought me?'

'A little money,' she answered, 'not much. I could not get much for you. I have had a quarrel with Mirelle—about you.'

'Have you brought me the diamonds?'

'No, and did not intend to do so; but I know where they are, and they are where you cannot get them.'

'Where is that?'

'In a very strong oak bureau in the room over the porch, and in a secret drawer in the well of that. That room cannot be entered except through the hall, main stairs, and Mirelle's bedroom. So put the thought of the diamonds out of your head. The bureau is always locked, and Mirelle keeps the key. Even if you got into the room, which is not possible, unobserved, you would not be able to open the cabinet. There—that is the end of that foolish dream, and I am glad of it. Had you taken them, I might have been suspected. I have had a quarrel with Mirelle—about you. But I must sit down moment, Sampson, and then run back.' She was out of breath; she spoke in short sentences, breathing hard between each. 'When we were together, she began to speak about the pendant she had given me, and to ask for it back. She said she would have the paste diamonds removed, and real stones put in their places. She told me that her necklace had been examined, and that it had been found that some only of the stones in it were false. A lady's maid of her mother had tampered with the jewels. Then she desired to compare my brooch, with its paste diamonds, with the real stones in her necklace; she got up and went to the bureau; she took the key out of her purse. There was a secret drawer opening out of a sort of well in the middle, and she brought the set of stones out of that. After that we had compared the false with the real diamonds she returned the necklace to its place, relocked the cabinet, and replaced the key in her purse. Then we began to speak about you. I told her that you were without any money, that you had lost everything in the ship, and had been further robbed by the men who saved your life. She asked what of?—of the stolen money? I then begged her to let you have something to help you to get away. She set her lips, and put on that stubborn look I know so well. She would give nothing. You had robbed Mr. Flamank and many others, and it was your duty to surrender yourself and suffer for your misdeeds. If you had any conscience and honour, that was what you would do, and she would not help you to evade the consequences of your own acts. My blood rose, and I spoke sharply. She was cold, hard, and obstinate. At last I got her to give me something, not for you, but for myself. She and her husband had made me a promise on their wedding day to give me some trifle, and I asked her if she purposed fulfilling that engagement, or whether it was only an empty promise. Then she replied that Herring had made the promise and would fulfil it, and that, if I was in immediate want of money, she would give me a small sum, all she could spare, for she had not more coin in the house. I was forced to be content. Here are twelve guineas; take them and be off. I can get you no more. There is no more to be got.'

'Well, Orange, I must take what I can get. The diamonds can wait. I have found something better than them in the locked drawer.'

'What is it, Sampson? Money?'

'No, not money. Do you like John Herring, Orange?'

'No.'

'I hate him,' said Sampson. 'You do not love Mirelle, I believe?'

'I hate her!' answered Orange, passionately.

'What I have found may serve to wipe off mutual grudges.'

'I am glad of it; use your knowledge.'

'I intend to do so on the proper occasion.'

'Well, good-bye, Sampson; I must return. Mirelle must not know that I have been here. I hope I have seen the last of you for some time.'

'I do not know. I must have a word with John Herring before I disappear entirely.'

O foolish Mirelle! Herring, before leaving, had laid on her two injunctions, to intrust no one with the secret of where she kept her jewels, and to allow no one to enter his office unattended by herself. She had disregarded and disobeyed both injunctions.

CHAPTER LI.

TWO EXITS.

John Herring said nothing to Cicely in allusion to what had passed. He could not do so. He was naturally reserved about himself, and he could not tell her of his marriage without telling her also of his separation from his wife. The questions would spring to her lips: 'When were you married? Why have you left her? Why are you now staying at West Wyke instead of at Welltown?' These were questions she would naturally ask, and which it would be impossible for him to explain to her. His trouble was his own. The heart knoweth its own bitterness, and a stranger intermeddleth not therewith. A woman delights in pouring forth her griefs into a sympathetic ear. A man hides his sufferings, and resents sympathy as an insult. Herring had said enough to let Cicely understand the position in which he stood towards her— that of a brother, a position he would never abandon; she had recognised this, and had accepted it.

Herring thought night and day of Mirelle. He could not shake the burden off his heart, and, whatever his distractions, it remained oppressing him, an ever-gnawing pain. He wondered what Mirelle was doing; whether she liked Welltown—that place he loved so well. When the sun shone out of a clear sky he thought, it is fine to-day at Welltown, and Mirelle will go upon the cliffs and hear the gulls scream and look at the twinkling sea; she will inhale that wondrous air which to him who breathes it is the inspiration of life in long draughts. Would she dare to go in a boat to Blackapit, when the sea was still, and look up those walls of inky rock striped with ledges on which the sea birds nested, up into the blue sky above, in which even by day stars can be discerned? Had she wandered to Minster Church, down in a valley embowered in trees, with the ruins of the old monastery crumbling about it? O how happy he would have been to be able to accompany her to the loved spots, wild and picturesque, that had been his delight in boyhood! Would she venture on an excursion to S. Kneighton's Kieve, and pick there the maiden-hair fern, dancing in the draught of the falling water? Would she visit Pentargon, that glorious cove with precipitous walls of rock black as night, over which a stream bounds in a long fall to meet the sea?

He thought of her sitting by the fire, in her white bridal dress, so lovely, so sad, so like a phantom, from another world. Mirelle haunted him. She filled his whole heart. Later, he would return to Welltown, when he and she had had time to realise the relation in which they stood to each other, and the first poignancy of the disenchantment was past.

Mirelle was to him the ideal of purity and perfection. He knew his own unworthiness. He was not the man who ought to own her as wife; he was rude and simple. She should be placed on a pedestal in a temple, to be approached by worshippers on bended knees. The snowdrops were out in the West Wyke garden. Herring plucked one every morning and wore it all day. Mirelle had worn snowdrops in her bosom when she married him. The snowdrop was her appropriate flower, white and fragile.

Herring was at Upaver all day. The mine was turning out better than even he had anticipated. There was no question now about the extinction of the debt on West Wyke. Mr. Battishill's profits would blot that out and redeem the mortgages. Mirelle's money sunk in the machinery would yield a dividend before the year was half out. Herring saw to everything himself. He inspired the men with energy. The contractor's bad work at the buildings was made good. His mind was occupied from morning to night; but he never forgot his trouble for one moment. It was ever there rankling in his heart: it took the gloss off success.

Mr. Battishill had sunk into a condition of mental feebleness and bodily exhaustion that engaged his daughter's constant attention. The old man could not be left alone. He no longer rose from his bed to take his old seat in the hall.

When Herring came back from Upaver, he went upstairs to the Squire's room, where he found Cicely knitting, and he sat there for an hour talking to the sick man, trying to interest him in what was going on at the mine. After dinner with Cicely in the hall, he went up again, and read Shakespeare to Mr. Battishill. The Squire was always ready for that. He had his favourite passages, and these he repeated after Herring, but his power to follow the movement of a scene and to distinguish characters was gone. Old familiar sentences caught his ear, and he murmured them after Herring, as he might follow a prayer, but his mind did not take in the sense. Yet he never wearied of this Shakespeare reading; it was like well-remembered melodies striking his ear and lulling him to sleep.

When the Squire had had enough, he always laid his thin hand across the book, and said in the words of Coriolanus, 'I am weary; yea, my memory is tired.' Then Cicely, John Herring, and Joyce knelt together by the old man's bed, and he folded his hands and said the one familiar prayer; and then Cicely and the rest bade him good night and left him.

Sometimes the old man would become uneasy, and ask John whether he would protect Cicely. 'You will always stand by her, will you not, John?'

Herring was obliged to give him the assurance he required.

'You are my children.'

'Yes, sir; brother and sister.'

'Brother and sister,' repeated Cicely.

Then the old man murmured, 'And she is fair, and, fairer than that word, of wondrous virtues.'

The Vicar of Tawton, the Reverend Harmless-Simpleton, was frequent in his calls. He was an amiable and well-intentioned man. The Simpletons are a large family, that have never thriven at the bar, in medicine, in the army and the navy, but the Harmless-Simpletons (the two surnames united by a hyphen) have for several generations made the Church their happy hunting ground. They have gone up in the Church like corks in water. The fattest livings, prebendal stalls, and even bishoprics have been showered upon them. As Napoleon won all his battles by one rule, so the Harmless-Simpletons acquired promotion by one simple principle. In the field of doctrine they never taught a truth without first treating it as a taxidermist treats a frog, killing, disembowelling, then blowing out the fleshless, boneless skin with wind, and varnishing the empty nothing. In the field of morals they never attacked a real enemy, but discharged their parks of ordnance, brought down charges of heavy dragoons, and displayed the most skilful strategy against imaginary foes.

When the Reverend Harmless-Simpleton called, he divided his visit into two parts, one of which was devoted to Mr. Battishill and the other to Miss Cicely, in the ratio of three to seven. Mr. Battishill was pleased to see and hear him, and Miss Cicely became deeply impressed with the reverend gentleman's amiability and good intentions.

So, little by little, the old Squire faded away.

There was another old man, who, much about the same time, made his exit from the stage, but in an altogether different manner.

Grizzly Cobbledick had been denied the linney in which to lie at night, 'like a heckamal in a haystack.' He was obliged, much as he objected to it, to return to the Giant's Table. As he feared that his old woman would be disposed to trouble his repose there, he provided himself with the means of sleeping soundly, in the shape of a stone jar full of spirits. Moreover, he paid a libation to her manes every night. He threw some drops of gin into the fire, saying, 'There, old cat! take that, and lie quiet.'

Grizzly was so far civilised by association with men that he knew the value of money. He had lost his shyness in the presence of men and his reluctance to appear in the neighbourhood of houses, and he would go into Zeal and hang about the taverns for drink and tobacco.

Now he had money of his own, and he launched into extravagance. He purchased a jar of Hollands, and carried it off with him to the Table, to comfort him at night—that he might lie in the straw and suck and nod, then suck and doze, open an eye and suck once more, and then drop off into a drunken stupor.

That which amused and puzzled him greatly was to see the spirit flame when he cast some drops on the lire. Water quenched fire: how came a liquor to leap into flame? This was more than his dull mind could take in. But it seemed to him that the essence of fire must be in the spirit, that was why it warmed him within, and danced and glowed in his veins. John Herring had been as good as his word. He had sent him straw, and the straw was heaped up at the back of the chamber.

'Take care, Grizzly,' said the man who brought him the bundles. 'Take care that your fire don't get to it; keep it well off.'

Grizzly had sense enough to do this. When he was sleepy the old man went backwards into the straw, disappearing entirely with the exception of his head and the hand that held the stone jar. The only firing was peat, and that did not flame.

When Herring cast him his purse, it was with the words: 'Some men cannot be helped. One must let them go to the devil their own way. You are one, and the sooner you go the better.'

Then Grizzly replied, 'I be going—I be a going as fast as I can.'

He kept his word. He went even faster than he intended, and the way he went was this.

He was sitting over the fire one evening. He had his stone jar under his arm, and he was patting it.

'Her be running dry, her be,' said he. 'Poor thing! let me hold'y up and try again.' He spoke to inanimate objects as though they were endowed with souls as reasonable as his own. 'There!' said he, as he cast a few drops on the fire, and laughed at the flames that leaped up; 'that be the blue blazes I've a swore by all my live and never knowed 'n, to see to, I reckon. Now there bain't another drop left. What ever shall I do? I have got more money, but no more spirits, and what be I to do all night long? Ah! I be a poor lorn creetur, I be. My old woman, her deserted me first, and a mighty shabby trick that were. Do'y hear me a speaking of 'y, old cat? Then my daughter Joyce, her left me —that is, I sold her when her'd a gone of herself. 'Twere good for me I got some money out of the deal: if I hadn't, her'd have cut and run all the same.' He sat and poked the red turves together. 'I wonder,' he said, 'what there be in thicky barrel I took from Ophir? Like enough there be first-rate drink in her. Old Tramplara weren't one to do things by halves. Her be hid away under the fern. I reckon I'll have her out and try.'

He groped beneath the straw to a nether layer of bracken, and from under that rolled a small keg.

'There ain't much comfort to be got out of she,' he said, 'her be so gashly small. I wonder what there be in her? Her be hard to open.'

He put the little barrel down by the fire.

'I reckon I could manage a hole wi' my old stone knife. Then he got the flint tool, and worked it between his palms on the end of the keg. The fire was getting low; he threw on some more turves. Then he ventured on a wisp of straw to make a blaze and assist his eyes.

'Oh, rallaluley!' he exclaimed, 'I've got the hole drilled through at last.'

He had stolen this little barrel from Ophir during the disorder occasioned by the discovery of the imposition. It was the only thing that he thought might possibly be of service to him. He took it away, and hid it under the fern at the back of the dolmen, intending to examine its contents at his leisure.

'Why, there be no drink here at all,' said he in disgust, when he had put his lips to the hole he had made. 'What be this? I've a got my mouth full of grit; it be black as coal. Blast me blue, but I will let my old woman taste it too.'

He let the contents run out in a little stream; then he gathered a handful of the grains and cast it in the fire to his 'old woman.' The contents of the keg then found their way out in a more expeditious manner than through the hole he had bored. The keg contained blasting powder.

Thus it came about that he fulfilled his promise faster than he had intended. Thus also it is that one of the most interesting monuments of a prehistoric age will not appear on the Ordnance Map of Devonshire now in process of execution.

CHAPTER LII.

THE RETURN OF THE WANDERER.

John Herring bad fulfilled his promise. He had made over five thousand pounds to Orange Tramplara. No sooner was this effected than it was whispered in the ear and the same day proclaimed on the housetops of Launceston. The proclamation reached Trecarrel. When Captain Trecarrel heard it, and had satisfied himself that this was not an empty report, he began to reconsider the state of his feelings towards Miss Orange. Five thousand pounds was a sum for which he might dispose of himself. It was not much, but more was not to be had in that neighbourhood. The Captain was without sisters and cousins scattered over the country, beating the covers for heiresses for him and blowing the horn when they had started one. He was forced to hunt for himself.

Five thousand pounds at five per cent. is two hundred and fifty pounds a year. Two hundred and fifty pounds per annum would enable him to keep his head above water—only his head, not his shoulders, but that would be better than to be overwashed by every wavelet. Now that old Mr. Tramplara was dead, there was no one to look closely after settlements—that was something. Captain Trecarrel was then in very particular want of money, and there was no money to be got through any other channel than the hymeneal ring. The property was already mortgaged, and the Captain could not encumber it further without cutting off his only means of subsistence.

He heard that Orange, followed after a fortnight by her mother, had moved to Welltown, near Boscastle, and was staying with Mr. and Mrs. Herring. The report was not quite accurate, for Mr. Herring, as we know, was not there. Report has the knack of interjecting into the best substantiated information an element of inaccuracy. He knew Herring, and thought that through him he might get the quarrel with Orange patched up—at least, through him he would obtain admission to the house where she lived. Herring would know nothing of the flirtation with Mirelle, and therefore would not scruple to admit him; and, once in, he would manage Orange. What girl could resist his handsome profile, his moustache and blue eyes!

Trecarrel knew that Orange loved him, and he knew also that when a woman loves, her pride and resentment give way whenever it pleases the lover to resume the assault. He would not be precipitate; he would be friendly at first, with a tinge of restraint and a savour of coldness in his manner towards her. This would yield by degrees, and they would soon recover their old intimacy and stand towards each other on the same footing as of old.

'I know perfectly well,' said the Captain, 'that there are hundreds, I may say thousands, of girls with fortunes who would give their ears for me, but the provoking thing is that they have never heard of me, nor can I obtain access to them. There are Birmingham and Manchester manufacturers' daughters, there are the girls of Bristol and Liverpool merchants, without family position, and with vulgar names, who would jump with all their moneybags into my arms, if I could only offer myself to them. But how am I to do so? I know nobody in Birmingham, Manchester, or Liverpool moneyed society, and I am unacquainted with any bridges. Between me and them there is a great gulf fixed, and though I would fain go to them, and they as gladly come to me, yet my tongue must parch in penury, and they must yawn in the bosom of Croesus. The means of intercommunication fail. I am getting on in life, I am thirty-four, and I ought to be doing something towards paying off my mortgages. I had rather have a girl with ten thousand than one with five, for then I should be twice as comfortable and connubial affection twice as strong; but if the girl with ten be not obtainable, I must be content with her who has only five. I wonder whence that five thousand came? I suspect old Tramplara put away money in his wife's name, and she has it; and that this five thousand has been placed to her daughter's account as a bait to draw me. If the old woman has money, it will come to Orange in the end; she is bad every winter with her throat, and this is a trying climate for throats, the temperature changes with such rapidity. The old woman would surely not be such a fool as to act the King Lear, and make over all she has to her daughter. She must have a reserve fund of at least five thousand more. By George, I'll risk it!'

So Captain Trecarrel took the Camelford coach as far as 'Drunkards all,' and walked from that point to Boscastle, making a man carry his valise. This was the cheapest way of travelling, and the Captain did everything as cheaply as he could, not because he liked it, but because he could not help himself. He put up at the Ship, where was a cosy little parlour and a clean bedroom. He would be comfortable there. He had brought his drawing materials with him, for the purpose of making water-colour sketches. When making his drawings he painted his subject in Indian ink, and then gave a Prussian blue wash to the sea, and a wash of Prussian blue and gamboge together over the grass and trees, and a wash of sepia to the rocks. Then he imagined a woman in a red cloak to be standing in a suitable position, and the picture would be complete. Gulls could be added 'to taste' by two little wet dabs with the brush and flicks with his handkerchief. When an evening light was wanted, by way of variety, the picture was submitted to a wash of pink-lake and gamboge in equal proportions. That was how water-colours were managed seventy years ago.

Captain Trecarrel sketched in the harbour, then he sketched in Willapark, and crept on to Welltown, where he found the old house so picturesque that he sketched it also. But the hedge was damp to sit on, so he ventured to the front door to borrow a chair, and having got one from Genefer he seated himself opposite the house, and began his drawing. He was a long time over it, as he was scrupulous about the details, and before it was completed Orange Tramplara came towards him. She was returning from Boscastle, where she had been making a few purchases. It was not possible for her to reach the front door without passing Trecarrel, and she had no hesitation in doing so, as she had no idea who was there sketching. He had an umbrella open to screen him from the wind; but there was a little hole in the umbrella, and through that he had perceived her. She was abreast of the Captain before she recognised him. He uttered an exclamation of surprise, started, and upset his sketchbook, box of colours, and glass of water into the road.

'I am very sorry, Captain Trecarrel,' said Orange, much agitated. 'I fear I knocked your things over with my cloak.'

'Not at all, Orange. Bless my soul! Who would have expected to see you here? In the name of all the seven wonders, what has brought you to this place, which I supposed was inhabited by wreckers only?'

Orange had recovered herself, and made as though she would pass on with a bow.

'No, Orange, I will not permit you to slip away thus. I want you to be in the foreground of my picture, as you have ever been in my thoughts. A marvellous piece of good fortune has brought us face to face. On a desert island those who have been cast up by the sea forget old grudges and shake hands. I will not be thrust aside in this wild and lonely spot, because once upon a time we had a lovers' quarrel.'

'I am surprised to see you here, Captain.'

'The surprise is mutual. I heard that you and Mrs. Tramplara had retired to Falmouth. Are you lodging at this old farmhouse for your mother's health?'

'This is Welltown, the house of Mr. Herring.'

'This! bless my soul! I thought he lived in a stately mansion in a deer park, not in an old ramshackle box like this. The world is smaller than I imagined. I have been making a sketching tour of the North Coast from Hartland to Boscastle, and I intend continuing it to the Land's End. I have some thought of publishing my sketches in mezzotint, coloured by hand. You know my impecuniosity. I thought to turn an honest penny this way without degradation.'

'Have you been long here?'

'Only a few days.'

'Where are you staying?'

'At the Ship.'

'What sort of entertainment do you meet with there?'

'Ham and eggs to-day; to-morrow, by way of variety, eggs and ham. Those are the changes. Nothing else is procurable all down the coast from Hartland to the Land's End. I am told, wherever I go, that next week a sheep or a cow will be killed, and then mutton-chop or beef-steak will be had. But the cow or sheep moves before me as I proceed on my journey, and I never overtake it.'

'We dine early. Will you join us?'

So peace was concluded. The difficulty in concluding it was not great, as Orange was as inclined to meet the Captain as he had been to meet her. Indeed, her readiness to strike hands and forget the past alarmed him. He was of a suspicious character, and her manifest desire to renew the old acquaintanceship made him dread a trap.

He did not know that Orange was getting deadly tired of Boscastle. Of society in the neighbourhood there was little. The only gentlefolks of county position were the Phyllacks of the manor. Old Sir Jonathan was a stately gentleman of the past generation, somewhat pompous, who moved surrounded by his seven daughters, as the judge encircled by the javelin men. The daughters were extraordinarily alike, and though the utmost effort had been made to distinguish them at the first by giving each two or three names, nevertheless Orange felt she might spend a lifetime in their company without being able to know Miss Grace Pomeroy from Miss Anna Maria Amy, or Miss Elizabeth Gilbert from either or from Miss Catherine Penhelligan. They never called separately, but called, all seven together, with Sir Jonathan in the midst. They never walked in batches, but walked in a system rotating round Sir Jonathan like the planets round the sun. When Mirelle and Orange returned their call, they found Sir Jonathan sitting at the fire in a hollow square composed by his daughters, and when one rose to shake hands, her place was occupied by another, whilst Sir Jonathan remained, bowing but inaccessible, behind their petticoats. The extraordinary thing about the Misses Phyllack was that they all seemed of the same age; their manners were alike, the expression of their faces equally sweet, the tones of their voices equally soft, like the cooing of wood-pigeons. They were all equally resolute never to admit a stepmother.

Even if Orange had contemplated it seriously, it was hopeless to break through this bodyguard of daughters, capture and carry off Sir Jonathan. After the call the old gentleman ventured to remark, 'A fine girl that!' whereupon Miss Grace Pomeroy objected that she was coarse, and Miss Anna Maria Amy that she had bad feet, and Miss Elizabeth Gilbert that she had a temper, and Miss Catherine Penhelligan that she was inelegant in her postures, and so on to the seventh, when Miss Grace Pomeroy took up the subject again, and poor Orange would have been picked to the bone, had not Sir Jonathan withdrawn his provocative remark with, 'Very true, my dears, very true; my eyes deceived me.'

Orange would have been glad enough to become Lady Phyllack, but to become Lady Phyllack the knight must be got at, and to get at him the circle must be broken. There was no Arnold of Winkelried at Boscastle to open a road through which Orange might dash in. Not a single Miss Phyllack had been lured from her post, all still were Misses Phyllack and coheiresses. It cannot be said that the ladies looked upon marriage as an evil to be avoided in their own persons, but, unfortunately for them, there were no marriageable young gentlemen in the neighbourhood. To find them they must go afield to Exeter or Bath, but to go there was to expose Sir Jonathan to fascinating widows and designing old maids; and though the knight occasionally suggested a migration to some fashionable resort, the daughters unanimously refused their consent, in their dread of it leading to a stepmother.

The seven young ladies received Mirelle readily into their society, but were cool towards Orange. The seven bosoms instinctively and together felt suspicious of Orange, and, after the remark their father had made, hostile towards her, as a dangerous person who must be kept out of Sir Jonathan's sight.

Orange had found that storm-beaten coast a very dull world. When Captain Trecarrel appeared in it, she felt relief and saw a chance of escape from it. Poor Mirelle was not prepared to receive the Captain with composure. The remembrance of what had passed between them on Christmas morning was too fresh, and she felt too keenly that it was her confession of love for him that had separated her from her husband, and would remain as a barrier keeping him away. She had been living a peaceful and lonely life at Welltown, and from seeing no more of Trecarrel her feelings towards him had become less intense. In time she hoped that this acuteness would be sufficiently blunted to enable her to think more of John Herring. She knew that it was her duty to love him, and she would try to do so, but to do so she must first forget Trecarrel. She was struggling with her heart, to hold it down, and bend it towards her husband. She allowed no thought to recur to Trecarrel. She shut her eyes against every flash of recollection that illumined him, as if to remember him were a sin. None suspected what was passing within, under that frozen exterior. She seemed wholly emotionless, and yet Orange knew that she was unhappy, was suffering, though she neither knew the extent nor the occasion of her suffering. Orange, who had never striven against any inclination or current of thought, had no suspicion of the systematic, deliberate, and obstinate battle Mirelle was fighting with her own heart.

And now, when the first resistance was broken, when she had gained some little successes, preludes of a complete victory, the Captain reappeared, introduced into the house by Orange to turn the scale of battle against her conscience. Mirelle received him with courtesy, but with coldness. She listened to his conversation without seeming to take interest in it, but out of civility she ventured to say a few words and ask a question, and directly dinner was over she withdrew to her boudoir with an apology, and without a request that he would renew his visit. Captain Trecarrel was a little disappointed at his reception. He had been profuse in his expressions of delight at accidentally renewing acquaintanceship, and had been pathetic on his distaste for ham and eggs alternating with eggs and ham.

When Mirelle left the hall, she hastened to her own room, and threw herself on her knees. The trial was more than she could bear. The sight of Trecarrel had undone in one moment the work of months.

Orange made amends for Mirelle's neglect. She begged the Captain to come there again for early dinner, whenever he was sketching in that direction; and as Captain Trecarrel found that the beauties of the portion of the coast south-west of Boscastle were superior to those on the north-east, he was there a good deal. He was surprised to find that neither Mirelle nor Orange knew anything of the sights of the neighbourhood. He volunteered to escort them. He insisted on taking them to S. Kneighton's Kieve, on driving them to Tintagel, and on their exploring the ruins of King Arthur's Castle together. They must visit Blackapit in a boat. There was a seal-cave that ought to be seen—it was a long way off and must be visited by boat—but the weather was splendid, and the sea was as calm as the Atlantic can be on this coast. The weather was indeed delightful, and the saddest heart could not resist the spring influence which swelled the buds and inspired the birds with song.

Mirelle allowed herself to be drawn on these excursions only with extreme reluctance. Orange was bent on going, and it was not proper to allow Orange to go alone with the Captain. A third person must accompany them, and Mrs. Trampleasure could not be induced to leave the house, her Blair's Sermons, and Rollin's 'Ancient History.' Mirelle felt that the place was dull for Orange, who, with her fulness of life and spirits, needed amusement. She was unable herself to provide her with distractions, and she therefore yielded to Orange's solicitations that they should accept the Captain's offers, and make these expeditions with him. But Mirelle hoped that each would be the last. The Captain was always on the eve of leaving to prosecute his tour, nevertheless there he remained. This was becoming unendurable to Mirelle; the strain on her was too great. Captain Trecarrel was very civil to Orange, but in her presence never more than very civil. Orange gave him every possible encouragement, but he still hesitated. He would not speak till he had sounded Mirelle as to the source and extent of Orange's property and expectations, and Mirelle never gave him the opportunity of speaking with her alone. Till he knew for certain what Orange was worth, and whether the five thousand pounds were really hers, or merely fluttered in his face to lure him on, he would not commit himself. Nor was this the only cause of his hesitation. Since he had come to Boscastle, he had heard of the Misses Phyllack, seven coheiresses, and he had done himself the honour of calling on Sir Jonathan. There was some remote connection between the families which justified him in paying a visit now that he was in the neighbourhood. He was graciously received by the young ladies, whose hearts were set in a flutter by his languishing blue eyes, and cordially by Sir Jonathan, who was delighted to have some one to talk to. So he dropped into the manor-house of an evening to take a hand at whist, and to talk about remote cousins, and to be an apple of discord among the seven sisters. If the seven Misses Phyllack had but one hand between them on which he could put the ring, Captain Trecarrel would not have hesitated to marry them all; but one out of seven coheiresses meant one seventh of Sir Jonathan's property when Sir Jonathan was dead, and the old knight looked remarkably robust; it meant also very little indeed, should the old gentleman marry again, and beget a son. Now, over the walnuts and wine one evening, when the daughters were out of hearing, Sir Jonathan had ventured on a remark about Orange: 'Fine woman that—deuced good-looking; my daughters won't let me look at a handsome face, but I may give them the slip some day.' This made Trecarrel uneasy, and next day he redoubled his attentions to Orange, and made no call at the manor.

Orange watched Mirelle, and saw that she loved Captain Trecarrel. She saw it in the struggle made by Mirelle to escape his society, by her reluctance to join in the excursions he proposed. Orange was suspicious of the Captain. Was he there for her sake, or because he was still attracted by Mirelle? She watched him closely. He was attentive to Mirelle, and his eye rested on her inquiringly now and then, when he thought he was unobserved.

Why, unless he still loved Mirelle, did he not ask Orange to be to him what she had been before? What stood in his way? That he was waiting till he knew all the particulars about her five thousand pounds, and till he had made up his mind about the Misses Phyllack, never occurred to her.

CHAPTER LIII.

A PRIVATE INTERVIEW.

For some time the stress of work at Upaver, and anxiety about both the success of the mine and the decline of Mr. Battishill's health, had kept under the yearning of John Herring's heart to see Mirelle again. Love was ever paramount, pain ever present, but he resolutely suppressed his desire to be with her. Duty kept him at West Wyke, and away from Welltown.

When, however, Mr. Battishill's life had ebbed away, and the first grief of Cicely was overpassed, and when Upaver mine was in full working order, when the spring was well on, and earth and sky were full of love, and joy, and hope, then the hunger of his heart became exacting. He must return to Welltown, see Mirelle, and may-be renew his pain.

The spring flowers were very lovely, and he brought bunches of them to Cicely; but that was not the same as offering them to Mirelle. It was pleasant to hear Cicely's gentle voice, with the faintest touch of Devonshire brogue in it; but that was nothing to the delight of listening to the tones of Mirelle's English tinged with French. He must see and hear her again. He could endure his banishment no longer.

The lodestone mountain drew ships to it, and when they came near extracted from them their bolts and nails, and the vessels went to pieces at its feet. Mirelle was his lodestone, and, even at the risk of a final and fatal wreck to his happiness, he must see her.

He still entertained the hope that in time Mirelle might learn to desire his presence, might come to think that life at Welltown would be pleasanter were he there to enliven it, might cease to shrink from him in that vague terror she had shown when he had told her his love, and when he had married her. She regarded him. Might not this regard deepen into a warmer sentiment?

Herring had told Cicely nothing. She had not made a second attempt to force her way into his confidence. It is difficult to say to what extent she suspected the state of his heart. She certainly had no knowledge of his marriage. Mirelle was never mentioned by either of them. He knew that Cicely instinctively disliked her, and she knew that he admired her, though she hardly suspected that he did more than greatly admire her.

Herring's position at West Wyke was anomalous. The people—that is, the workmen at the mine, and the farmers and cotters on the estate—called him the young Squire, and supposed that he was a near relative, and the heir to the property. They sometimes spoke of him as young Squire Battishill. There were few neighbours of the class of the Battishills, and those that were had long ceased to call on the old gentleman and his daughter. They themselves were mounting in the world, and the Battishills were falling. He gave no entertainments, and kept no carriage, not even a gig. This class therefore did not concern itself with the affairs at West Wyke, after it had done the civil thing of attending his funeral. Nevertheless John Herring felt that the situation was unsatisfactory. He would have liked to take Cicely to Welltown to stay with Mirelle, for change of air and scene, and to have persuaded Mirelle to return with them to West Wyke, when he was recalled by the concerns of the mine. But, as matters stood between him and his wife, this was not possible.

At times he fell into a daydream, which brightened his spirits for a few hours. He thought that perhaps now Mirelle might bid him stay by her. Then his future would be changed, the spring would burst forth in his heart, as in surrounding nature. Till then the frost must lie within. He must go home and learn his fate. He could stay away no longer. No—no! West Wyke was not home. He must see if the ice were thawing at Welltown.

So he bade farewell to Cicely and Joyce, set the men at Upaver their tasks, and departed.

There was another motive in his heart drawing him back to Welltown— another beside his desire of again seeing Mirelle. In the locked drawer of his office desk he had left his confession to Mirelle—his confession of the fact that all the money that had been spent to buy up the West Wyke mortgages, that had been sunk in Upaver, and that which had been given to Orange, and that also which Mirelle was now enjoying, was her own, the proceeds of the sale of the uncut diamonds her father had brought to England from Brazil— the diamonds in which he had invested his fortune as a convenient and portable form in which to transfer it from one country to another. He did not wish Mirelle to see this. He did not wish it, for his own sake and for hers. For good or for ill—it seemed wholly for ill—the thing had been done, and could not be recalled. By no means could the effects of the mistake be avoided. If she knew the circumstances, nothing she could do would alter them, and the knowledge would only give her additional and renewed pain, for she might well suppose that had it come to her earlier she would have been saved from taking the fatal step that could not now be retraced. Putting his own wishes aside entirely, Herring could see that the only chance of happiness open to Mirelle was for her to accept the situation, draw towards him, and learn to love him. Were the truth now to break on her, the breach would become irreparable. He knew that he had acted towards her unselfishly and conscientiously, and the error into which he had fallen had been an error of judgment. But would she believe this? Was it not far more probable that she would suppose he had acted with selfish premeditation from the first, and thus become for ever embittered against him?

His anxiety about the confession grew as he thought this over and fevered him as he walked. He resolved directly on his arrival to destroy the document. Why had he not done so before instead of leaving it? Because he had been flurried at leaving, and had thought that it might be useful on some future occasion. The drawer was locked, and therefore he had no cause for fear, but nevertheless he was uneasy. Other keys besides his own might unlock it, and though he did not believe that Mirelle would wilfully and knowingly pry into what he wished to keep concealed, yet it was possible that his words relative to the locked drawer when he left her had been unheeded, and that, finding a key wherewith to open it, she might look in for some mislaid paper or account needed by the foreman of the slate-quarry, and when the drawer was opened she would see the packet lying in it addressed to herself. Herring went accordingly to Willapark first, and with his private key unlocked the office, and then locked himself in. The office was much as he had left it, and yet not entirely. Some one had been there. The chairs were in unusual places. The position of the desk was changed. Probably Genefer had done this in dusting or cleaning. He opened the drawer immediately, and saw that the packet was gone.

Herring sat down on his bed to think. He was almost certain that the letter had been put in the locked drawer, and yet, when he came to revolve in his mind the events of the night and morning when the letter had been written and put away, he found that he could be certain of nothing about it save that he had written, made up, and addressed the packet. He had purposed putting it in the drawer and locking it up. He believed he had done as he purposed, but it was possible that, in the confusion and distress in which he then was, he might have omitted to do so. If the letter had been put elsewhere, it must have been put in his cupboard. This cupboard consisted of a set of shelves that had been run up in a recess, combined with an extemporised wardrobe, where he kept his suit in which he went out boating and shooting.

The cupboard was not closed with a door, but had a curtain on an iron bar in front of it, which latter turned on a crook. He went at once to this closet and thrust the bar and curtain aside so as to get into the recess and examine the shelves. To this place he had gone for the bullets on that turning night in his life. He mounted a stool to explore the upper shelves. He would not leave one unsearched till he had found the missing packet. Whilst thus engaged he heard a key put into the lock, and the door opened. He was surprised, and remained where he was, screened from view.

Then he heard Mirelle say: 'Captain Trecarrel, I sent for you to meet me here in private, as I have something to say to you which I do not wish Orange to hear, because it concerns Orange.'

'Mirelle,' replied the Captain, 'I also have been desirous of seeing you in private, as I also have something to say to you which is not for Orange's ears.'

The first impression on Herring's mind on hearing these words was surprise at Mirelle's indiscretion in arranging a private interview with the Captain. Not a shadow of suspicion of other motives than what were honourable crossed him. It had never occurred to him that Trecarrel was the man Mirelle loved. Had he known this, nevertheless not a thought of anything unworthy of her would have entered his mind. He saw that she had acted in ignorance of conventional proprieties. His first impulse was to step forward and show himself. On second thoughts he refrained from doing so. He refrained for Mirelle's own sake. If he were suddenly to emerge from behind the curtain it would bring home to her at once the impropriety of her conduct, embarrass and distress her, and place both her and the Captain in a very awkward position. The interview was about Orange, and there could be no reason why he should not overhear it, and indeed take part in it, unless it were, as he supposed, concerning the Captain's engagement to Orange. If that were so it would be kindest to allow Mirelle to have her few words about it with Trecarrel, and he—John Herring—would tell her immediately after that he had overheard the conversation.

'Je vous donne le pas, Monsieur le Capitaine.'

'Je le prends de bon gré, madame,' replied Trecarrel. 'But as I think in English and not in French, perhaps you will allow me to say what I want in my native tongue.'

'Certainly.'

'In the first place, then, let me speak about my book on the Cornish Coast scenery. I think it advisable that you should possess early copies—proofs before the plates are worn. I think you offered to take three copies at five guineas.'

'I believe I did. Have you secured a publisher?'

'No, not yet, but that is a matter of secondary importance. A publisher can always be secured for drawings such as mine, of scenery that has such historic interest—King Arthur, Uther Pendragon, Gwenever, and so on.'

'No doubt.'

'If not inconvenient to you, would you mind letting me have your subscription at once? I want, you understand, to secure you unrubbed copies.'

'You shall have the money to-morrow.'

'You quite see that I am pressing this entirely in your own interest. There is a material difference between early copies and late impressions, and first subscribers who have paid up will, as a matter of strict justice, be given the best and sharpest copies.'

'Quite so.'

'There was another matter on which I wished to speak to you. A man was saved from the wreck of the "Susanna" in the winter. That man gave out his name as George Bidgood. You, I understand, gave him shelter. You are aware who he is?'

'I saw him brought ashore.'

'You know then that he is no more George Bidgood than I am. George Bidgood was the seaman on board the "Susanna," and was lost in it. The man who was rescued from the waves was Sampson Tramplara, but, as he desired to disguise the fact that he had been saved and was alive, he took for the occasion the name of the drowned man, and there was no one in Boscastle who knew otherwise except yourself. Sampson disappeared after that, but he has just turned up again, as it happens, at an awkward moment for himself, for the "Chough" has come into harbour, and the mate of the "Chough"—a little smack that trades between this place and Bristol—knew Bidgood intimately, and the same man had learned in Bristol that a swindler had made off in the "Susanna," and was supposed to have been lost in her. Last night Sampson was at the Ship Inn drinking, when the mate of the "Chough" came in and joined the party. In the course of conversation Sampson was spoken of as Bidgood; this led to an explanation, and then the mate charged him with being the man whom justice was pursuing, disguising himself under Bidgood's name. There was a disturbance, Sampson was drunk, and in the scuffle he stabbed the mate, and made his escape.'

'Mon Dieu! le pauvre homme! est-il mort?'

'No. The man is not dead, but he has been mortally wounded. However, the condition of the mate concerns us only in a secondary manner—the fate of Sampson is that with which we have to do.'

'He must suffer for what he has done.'

'Will you speak to Orange, and tell her what has taken place?'

Mirelle hesitated a moment, and then said, 'If necessary I will do so.'

'It is necessary. Sampson must not be taken here. The mate is mortally wounded; Sampson must be helped to escape. If he wants money and means of escape he must be provided with them.'

'I will not assist him with money or means of escape. He has done wrong, and must take the consequences.'

'You are right, no doubt, in principle, but the world cannot go on upon principle, it must have its workings eased to suit convenience. It will never do that he should be taken here, and your relationship to the scoundrel come out.'

'It cannot be helped.'

'But you must consider Orange and her mother. By the way, there is another matter I must mention. I have had a talk with Sampson—of course, before this last unpleasant affair with the mate of the "Chough." He was not shy of me, for he knew I would not betray him. During our conversation he let drop some insinuations against your—against Mr. Herring. He says that Mr. Herring robbed you of the greater portion of your fortune, without either you or Mr. Tramplara, your guardian, knowing or suspecting it.'

'Stop,' said Mirelle, haughtily; 'not another word, Captain Trecarrel. Mr. John Herring is incapable of acting otherwise than honourably, and I refuse absolutely to listen to slanders that issue from the mouth of Sampson Trampleasure.'

'You are right, Countess, quite right. I was as indignant as you are now. I positively refused to believe it. But he proceeded to enforce his hints with circumstances.'

'Captain Trecarrel, you must have understood me very imperfectly. I refuse to hear another word on this offensive and insulting topic. If you have done speaking about the escape of Mr. Sampson Trampleasure, let me say what I desire to say. Mr. John Herring is an honourable man, and in his absence I am the guardian of his honour.'

'I also shut my ears when Sampson said what he did,' continued Captain Trecarrel; 'I had no intention of saying anything to you about the reflections he cast on the character of your husband which might be disagreeable for you to hear, I mention this only as supplying an additional reason for getting Sampson Tramplara out of the way, even by helping him with money. It would be most unpleasant for you were he to make disclosures affecting John Herring's character——'

'He can make no such disclosures. John Herring's character cannot be impeached.'

'Certainly—I used the wrong term: were he to hint——'

'The hints of such as he can do no harm.'

'There you are wrong; they would be eagerly listened to, and believed. John Herring is not here to defend himself, and as you say you are the guardian of his honour, I think it is your duty to save him this annoyance.'

'If that be so, let him escape. It goes against my conscience, but, to save my husband unpleasantness, I will do what you ask. I will give him money. You may take my purse.'

'Excuse me. I shall not see the fellow. He is not likely to show again at the Ship, nor am I likely to come across him anywhere in my walks. But he will not leave without having seen Orange. She must have provided him with money before, and his return to Boscastle now means that he has spent all she let him have, and wants more.'

'I will speak to Orange, and give her money. But now that this hateful subject is settled, you will allow me to speak to you about Orange.'

'I am ready to hear anything you may say.'

Mirelle hesitated. She began to tremble, and cast her eyes on the ground. 'Orange,' she began—'that is to say, I mean—but, Captain Trecarrel, it is hard for me to say what I want, and you ought not to have put the necessity on me of saying it. You are not acting fairly by Orange, or—by me. I am sure that—that Orange regards you very, very much; you were engaged to marry her, and I think—I do think you are bound in honour to do so. She is not happy; I can see that she frets. You are trifling with her heart. Why are you here? Why do you not prosecute your journey? Time presses; you must finish your series of sketches whilst the fine weather lasts. Why, then, do you remain here, and come up to Welltown every day, and make excursions with us, and—why do you not leave us in peace?'

'You, you, Mirelle, urge me to make Orange Trampleasure my wife after ——'

She cut him short. 'You are bound to marry her. Do you not see that yourself? You were engaged to her before that miserable affair of Ophir intervened to destroy her happiness.'

113

'After what I told you, Mirelle, that Christmas Day?'

'Forbear!' said Mirelle; 'never recur to, nor allude to that again. I have forgotten it—that is, I try, I pray to forget it. Yes, I entreat you to take Orange.'

'There are several objections,' said Trecarrel. 'In the first place, I cannot afford it.'

'Orange has five thousand pounds.'

'Has she no more?'

'Not that I am aware of.'

'What puzzles me is, how did she come by the money? I thought everything had gone when that scamp Sampson bolted.'

'That is easily explained. John Herring gave her the money.'

'He gave Orange five thousand pounds! This is incredible. What claim had she on him?'

'She had been kind to me. I asked him to do it.'

'An exemplary husband! But how the deuce did he come by so much money? I know what Welltown is worth. He cannot have saved it—men in the army spend, they do not save; he cannot have made it. He did not inherit it. Whence did it come?'

'That concerns neither you nor me to know.'

'Orange then really has, of her own, five thousand pounds.'

'Yes.'

'Has she prospects of more?'

'I believe not.'

'Five thousand pounds! By the way, would it be possible to organise a picnic conjointly with the Misses Phyllack to Crackington Cove? The old knight to stay at home.'

'Captain Trecarrel, you are evading the point. You are trying to turn the subject. I am anxious; I am troubled. Do not play with me. It cost me a severe struggle to make up my mind to speak to you alone, and on this subject.'

'Why should it cost you a struggle?'

'It has—that is enough. Do you not see? I am pleading for a—a sister; for her happiness. Can you not understand that I am shy of doing this, and that I only do it as a duty, and for the sake of a sister?'

'Mirelle!' said the Captain, slowly. He looked hard at her. 'That is not it. I can read your heart more clearly than you think. You are desirous of getting me to marry Orange so as to erect a double wall of duty between yourself and me—it is because you doubt your own fortitude unless double-steeled with a sense of twofold duty——'

'Captain Trecarrel!' exclaimed Mirelle, in deadly terror—for he had divined and given expression to her real motive. 'I pray you say nothing about me. Put me altogether out of your thoughts. Speak only of Orange.'

'You see there is this confounded business about Sampson in the way. Suppose the fellow be apprehended—and the whole of Boscastle is alive and out after him—and suppose the mate dies, as is most probable, Sampson will swing. Do you not see that I cannot well quarter the chevronels with a gallows?'

'He shall escape—he must escape. Orange shall have the money! Captain Trecarrel, either take Orange, or go your way to the Land's End.'

'I want time to consider.'

'Take time, but not too much. Now leave me.'

'Oh, Mirelle, is not this cruel of you—of you who knew the state of my heart, what I have suffered, and am suffering still—

'Leave me!' said Mirelle. She trembled in every limb. 'Leave me!—leave me!'

He hesitated a moment, and then went out.

She stood looking at the door. Then her pent-up feelings burst forth. She cast herself on her knees, and sobbed and cried, 'My God! my God! forgive me! I love him still! I have striven against it! Thou knowest the secrets of the heart. I love him still!' Then the door burst open, and Orange came in, her face livid with rage, and her large eyes flashing hate.

'What is this?—is this?—you meet Captain Trecarrel in secret and alone here?'

'I beg your pardon, Miss Trampleasure,' said Herring, stepping forward; 'not in secret, nor alone. I have a right, I presume, to see any one or two in my own room that I choose.'

Mirelle looked up dazed. Her eyes were blind with tears. She understood nothing of what was going on, neither how Orange had come in, nor whence Herring had risen.

Orange looked first at Herring, then at Mirelle, still kneeling and with tears in her eyes and on her cheeks, and laughed scornfully.

'I apologise, Mr. Herring. I have intruded on the confession of a penitent.'

CHAPTER LIV.

THE PORCH ROOM.

Herring gave his arm to Mirelle to conduct her back to Welltown. He did not say much to her, as his own heart was full, and she, he knew, needed time to recover herself.

Now he knew all. He had never suspected an attachment for the Captain, but had supposed that she had lost her heart to some one in France. What he now learned increased his trouble. Separation from a lover on the other side of the Channel might, in time, have effaced or obscured his image, but Trecarrel was too near to be forgotten. Herring saw that Trecarrel had perceived that Mirelle's efforts to bring about a reconciliation and re-engagement with Orange were dictated by alarm for herself, by her desire to erect a double barrier between herself and the man she loved, so as to afford her conscience a double reason for mastering her affection for him.

Herring did not wish to speak with Mirelle on this subject till later—till he had had time to think over the situation in which he and she were now placed. He therefore said a few words on ordinary topics during the walk to Welltown. He observed that she seemed even frailer and more bloodless than before. The strong air of the coast had not braced her into vigorous life, but seemed to overpower the feeble life that pulsated in her veins.

'You do not grow stronger, Mirelle?'

'I am well in body,' she said.

'I do not think so. You ought to see a doctor—you look so thin and white.'

117

'The only doctor I need is the sun,' she answered, 'and his visits are so few that they must be costly.'

'But this wonderful stimulating air——'

'There is too much air. It is never at rest—always blowing. I dislike the wind. And the sea is always tossing and thundering. The leaves on the plants, the blades of grass, are never still, but always fluttering and swaying. The waves are ever battering and gnawing at the rocks. O for a Mediterranean—a tideless sea! I want peace, stillness, a calm; with the sun shining, and no sea near, and no noise save the hum of bees. Here there are no bees; the wind carries them out to sea and they drown in the brine. You do not understand me. Here there are no butterflies; the wind breaks their wings. You do not comprehend my state of mind.'

'Yes, I think so. You like a hot climate.'

'I love warmth, but I love stillness better. That is what my soul craves for and cannot obtain. Here the flowers do not bloom—they blow away. Here the birds do not sing—they scream. Here we have weeks of gloomy skies. I want no shadow at all save that of a cross flung over a hot white road. But one sees no crosses here, only signposts. We bear our own crosses hammered red-hot into our lives.'

The evening was beautiful. The sun was setting over the sea, making a road of quivering gold upon the waves. The air was warm. Herring looked round. The scene was grandly beautiful. He wondered that Mirelle could not love it.

He went into the house, and had tea in the hall with her and Mrs. Trampleasure. Orange feigned a headache and did not appear.

Then he ascended the stairs with Mirelle to the little boudoir or porch room; he must have a conversation with her in private before again leaving.

The room was small; it was pleasant, prettily furnished with rose-coloured satin curtains, the walls white and gold. But the damp had come through the paper and formed black fungoid stains, disfiguring all one side. There was no fireplace in the room, so that it could only be used in summer. In the corner stood the bureau in which Mirelle kept the jewels, a bureau of inlaid wood, with ornamental brasswork about the locks and handles. The chairs were white and gold. Herring had spent a good deal of money on this room, hoping that it would please Mirelle, and that she would be happy in it.

He took a chair. She seated herself in the window on the low seat. She opened the casement, and the summer air was wafted in, bearing on its wings the murmur of the sea.

'Mirelle,' he said, 'I overheard all that passed in the office on Willapark. I was there when you came in, but I did not show myself, lest by so doing I should cause you embarrassment. Excuse my saying it, but I do not think you acted wisely in inviting Captain Trecarrel to meet you there.'

'No, I do not think I did, but I could not in any other way get a word in private with him.'

'And you wished to urge him to marry Orange. I think with you that in honour he is bound to take her.'

'Yes, I wish that very much.'

'At the same time I think your interference ill-calculated to advance the cause you have at heart. It was indiscreet of you, Mirelle.'

'Perhaps so. You are always right, and know what ought to be done, and do it.' After a pause, she said: 'Yes, it was not wise of me. I will never do it again. But then, consider, I was alone, and had no one to advise me, for in this matter I could not consult Orange. When I was at the Sacré Coeur, I knew my way about the dear home in the dark, but here I am in a world without orientation. All the familiar landmarks fail me, all the ways lead in unknown directions. I am translated, morally, into a country that I am expected to travel through without a map or a guide.'

'Mirelle, if you like, you have only to say the word and I will stay here as your adviser. You are too weak.'

'No, my good friend, I am not weak.'

'Weak in body, Mirelle—not weak in character.'

'No; I will always do my duty, as I see it.'

'You are too inexperienced to be left alone.'

'I have Orange with me.'

'But what is Orange as an adviser? You confessed as much just now when you admitted you were without a guide. Mirelle! I am sure Orange does not like you. She is'—he was about to add 'jealous,' but he checked himself —'she is not a desirable person to have about you perpetually. I do not trust her sincerity.'

'I do. I have never done anything to make her dislike me.'

He remained silent. It was difficult for him to speak the truth, and yet it must be spoken for her sake.

'Orange is strongly attached to Captain Trecarrel; that you know,' said Herring. 'Now a loving woman is a suspicious woman. He will not renew his engagement with her, he shirks doing so; and she seeks an explanation of his conduct, and finds it where she has no right to look for it.'

Mirelle turned her face to Herring.

'I told you all, that evening after we had been married. You know that something passed between him and me, not much, just enough to——'

'Yes, Mirelle, you told me that your heart was a treasure I might not possess, but you did not inform me to whom you had surrendered it.'

'I did not! I failed in my duty. I intended to do so, my friend.'

'You did not, but now I have found it out.'

'Oh, John Herring, do not say that I surrendered my heart. That I never did. It was drawn from me, and I fought against it, I prayed against it. God help me! I have been very miserable: I am miserable still. You are not angry with me? I could not help myself.'

'I—I angry with you? No, Mirelle, never; you have done me no wrong. If wrong has been done, it has been done by me to you.'

'I have suffered, because since I married you I knew it was wrong to think of another man, and I do believe I should have conquered in the end had not Captain Trecarrel come here. I thought he came after Orange, and I have done my best to promote her interests. I want him to go away, and then I will begin my battle over again. He will leave now, and in time I shall have conquered the thoughts I ought not to harbour.'

'Mirelle—one word. Shall I stay here? I shall not trouble you with my presence more than is absolutely necessary. My old office shall be my home, but I shall be at hand to advise and to help you.'

She shook her head.

'I have no right to say Go, or Stay. You must act as you see fit. You are master here; you are my husband; this is your house. But if you will listen to my prayer, I will ask you to go away again—not for long, for a little while. I want rest; I want to be quite alone with God and my own heart. I have got a wrestle to go through, and I had rather undertake it without a spectator. Do not be afraid for me. I shall come out victorious in the end, I do not doubt that. Only, these wrestles take a great deal of strength out of me. When I feel better, and know that the worst is over, I will write to you, and then come and I shall be able to see you. You are still my friend—nothing I have said or done has altered that?'

'No, no—Mirelle.'

'I always respect and honour you. I know that you are upright and good, and I would love you if I could. I may do so some day, but the weed must be rooted out before the grain is sown.'

'Very well, Mirelle. You said as we walked back from Willapark that here we have the cross hammered into our lives. You have yours, I have mine. It must be so. Perhaps a better time may be in store for both of us.'

'Perhaps.' She looked sadly out of the window. The sun had set, and the golden path on the sea was turned to quicksilver. She rose and moved towards the door into her own room.

'I am very tired. Shall we say Good night?'

'And good-bye. I leave before morning.'

'It is best so.'

She hung about the door, looking timidly at him. Her hand was on the latch, and it shook; she removed it, but presently put it on again.

'When am I to return? In a month, or two months?' he asked.

She shook her head. 'I cannot say; I will write to you. Give me your address before you leave.'

'There are one or two little matters connected with our affairs here that ought to be discussed.'

'Here is the key of my bureau. Will you write your instructions? They shall be carried out faithfully. I am very tired. You said I was weak; I am weak in body. Write at my desk, and leave the note in it, and the key in the lock.'

'Very well, Mirelle; good-bye!'

Then she raised her great dark eyes to him, and came tremblingly towards him.

'Kiss me,' she said; 'you have a right to that.'

He took her pale face between his hands, and reverently kissed her cheek, and a salt tear off it was received by his lips. He knew that she did not love him. He knew that her cheek was offered him only because of the strong sense of duty at her heart, and because she felt that some reparation was due for the bitter pain she had caused him.

When he had let her go she bowed her head, and with lowered eyes and a hectic spot of colour on the cheek that he had touched, without another word or look, she disappeared through the door.

Herring sat for a few moments with his hands over his face, and then went to the bureau, opened it, and, taking some paper, wrote on it his address, and various memoranda relative to the house and quarry. When he had done he closed the desk, turned the key, descended the stairs, and left the house. As he went through the gate he thought he saw a man behind the wall near the entrance to the yard, and, supposing this was Hender, Herring cast him a good-night. There was no reply, but this caused him no surprise; Hender was a surly man, not addicted to the courtesies of life. Herring did not give him another thought; he had enough to trouble his mind without care for Hender's manners.

His conversation with Mirelle had been, in a measure, satisfactory; as satisfactory as he could expect. There was some faint hope before him; she was doing her best to overcome that unfortunate passion which stood as a dividing wall between them. Time would assist her efforts, which Herring knew were sincere, and then perhaps she might come to care for him. She valued him now; she had not shrunk from him as before, but had freely volunteered a kiss. She had assured him that but a short while would elapse before she would recall him. When the weed was eradicated then the corn would grow. The hope set before him was not a great one; still it was something to have a hope at all. He went back to Willapark, resolved to examine the quarry accounts, write instructions to the captain, and depart that night on his return to West Wyke. He would walk back, and therefore not go by Launceston, but strike across country into the Holsworthy and Okehampton road.

Not many minutes after Herring had left Welltown, that man whom he had observed behind the yard wall crept forth with a ladder that he had taken from an outhouse. He looked cautiously about him, and then planted the ladder noiselessly against the porch. He threw off his shoes, and swiftly ascended. The window of the boudoir was open, as Mirelle had left it, and the man lifted himself in through it. He stole across the room over the soft carpet to the bureau. The sky was full of twilight, and everything in the room could be distinguished. The window faced north, and the northern sky was illumined with silvery light. A streak of yellow light beneath the door showed that Mirelle's candle was burning in her bedroom. The man listened. He heard steps coming along the passage. Then a door was opened. It was that into the adjoining bedroom, and a voice was heard speaking. The man smiled; he knew the voice well, it was that of Orange Trampleasure, and she was speaking to Mirelle.

Then he turned the key in the bureau, opened it, and searched the well. He soon found the secret drawer, and removed from it the diamonds. He was about to close the desk when he noticed the papers Herring had written, his address, and memoranda. The man caught these up hastily, and then with a low, bitter laugh, and a look full of malignity in the direction of Mirelle's door, he put in their place the packet containing Herring's confession to his wife, written the night of his marriage, and stolen from his drawer by Sampson Tramplara. That man who now placed the letter where Mirelle must find it was the same who had stolen it—Sampson Tramplara.

All this was the work of a few minutes. As rapidly as he had ascended the ladder and entered the room, so did he descend, replace the ladder where he had found it, and disappear.

CHAPTER LV.

NEMESIS.

John Herring was engaged on the accounts in the office for some hours.

Whilst thus engaged he heard the door open behind him, and, when he turned to look who had come in, saw Sampson Tramplara.

'What brings you hither?' he asked, springing to his feet, and flushing with anger.

'What brings me hither?' repeated Sampson, and laughed. 'You, Mr. John Herring. I want a quiet talk with you.'

'Go away at once; I have nothing to say to you.'

'But I have something to say to you, Mister John. In the first place, I want a change of clothes.'

'You must go elsewhere for them.'

'No, I am going nowhere else. I have set my heart on a boating suit hanging in yonder cupboard, or wardrobe, or whatever you call it. I have come for that. There are reasons that prevent my appearing in public, and in the costume that I now wear, becoming though you may think it. Those reasons are, that if I am seen, I shall be arrested, first for that confounded Ophir, and secondly, because last night I stuck a knife into a man with whom I had a brawl in a tavern. So now I call you to find me the suit of clothes in which I may escape. The reason, because it is not to your advantage that I should be taken here. Remember, I am the cousin of your wife; you have married into my family. Mirelle gave me shelter when shipwrecked, and though she knew who I was, like a sensible girl, she held her tongue. My mother and sister are your guests. If you refuse me clothes, I shall go to your house, and be taken there, in the society, in the presence, of Mrs. John Herring and her cousins. That will be nice and creditable to the family, will it not? That will be highly entertaining to the ladies, will it not? I reckon that fellow whom I stuck will hardly recover, and if he dies I must swing for it. Creditable to the family, to be able to boast of Cousin Sampy who was gallowsed. I suppose I shall be hung in chains here. Pleasant to have a cousin of Mrs. John so exalted within a sniff whenever she walks abroad.'

'Take the clothes you want,' said Herring; 'be quick, and be off.'

Tramplara went to the recess, and took the garments he required, and proceeded to divest himself of his own clothes, and invest himself in Herring's boating and shooting suit.

'They fit me as if made for me,' said Sampson. 'A good substantial suit this. And here is J.H. on the buttons; that is in style. Look at me. We are the same height, and about the same build; we have about the same coloured hair. It is a d—d pity that I have not your luck. I want something more now.'

Sampson proceeded to roll up his old suit.

'It will not do to leave these garments about; they would betray my change of skin. I must throw them over the cliffs. It is a fortunate thing that there are no sands here on which a bundle confided to the waves can be washed ashore. Here the waves and rocks worry what is given them past all recall, within a surprising short time. Look at me. This suit becomes me. We might be brothers. Now, brother John, I want something wherewith to line the pockets, which I find are empty.'

Whilst talking, Sampson transferred the contents of the pockets of his old coat to the breast pocket of the waistcoat of his new suit—an inner pocket. As he did so he laughed, and looked contemptuously at Herring, who was not observing him. That which he transferred was the case containing Mirelle's diamonds. He put that in the inner pocket of his waistcoat, which he buttoned tightly over it.

'Look here!' said he; 'this is all the cash I have, a crown and a halfpenny. Is a crown and a halfpenny enough to carry me across Cornwall and out of England? I want some blunt, and I will trouble you to find me some.'

'Go along, you scoundrel! It is enough for me to have allowed you my old clothes—I will give you no further assistance.'

'That is a pretty name to give me—scoundrel! Pray what reason have you for thus entitling me?'

'Every reason. You and yours robbed Mirelle of what her father had left.'

Sampson laughed.

'Oh, this is beautiful! Virtuous innocence condemns impenitent vice. Brother John, we are both in the same box. It don't become you to ride the virtuous horse; it trots beautifully along a smooth road, but I think I can lay something in its way will trip and tumble it over. You have had your pickings, and a d—d richer find yours was than mine.'

Herring looked at him speechless. Was this a random shot, or did he know anything?

'You are a proper person to act the moral character. James Strange left my father sole trustee of everything, did he not? How much of all he left did you allow him to finger, eh? How much did you keep back for yourself?' Sampson paused for a reply. He stood opposite Herring, with his hands on his hips. 'Don't you think it possible that Cousin Strange, in leaving Brazil, sent over as much ready money as he thought he might want, and put the bulk of his property into diamonds, which he could dispose of in London at any time? By his will he constituted my father sole trustee of everything—that is, of money and diamonds. My father never caught sight of the diamonds, never laid a finger on one of them, for a very good reason, they were stolen by virtuous John Herring.'

'This is false.'

'No, it is true. You did not rummage the trunk of Cousin Strange, or take them out, that I'll allow; but you received the stolen jewels, and the receiver is as bad as the thief, is he not?'

Herring could not speak.

'My father was constituted trustee. If you had been honest, when you received these diamonds you would at once have taken them to him. You were not honest. You kept them.'

'Sampson Trampleasure, I kept them only for Mirelle, in her interest. I knew the character of your father, I knew what he was doing with the rest of

127

the money intrusted to him, and I would not risk the rest of her property.'

'Who authorised you to keep it?'

'I acted as my conscience directed.'

'Conscience!' exclaimed Sampson, derisively, 'I like to hear that word pleaded; it always means, when interpreted, self-interest. Some men follow their consciences as a gardener follows a wheelbarrow, by pushing it along before him. Answer me, would the law have authorised you to keep back the diamonds?'

'No; the law would not.'

'Then who authorised you? Did Mirelle? Did you consult her about them? I am at a loss to know what other authorisation you could find.'

'No, I did not speak of them to her—and that for reasons of my own.'

'No, I know you did not. You acted on what you call conscience, and I, self-interest. I will tell you what you did with Mirelle's money. You were soft and sweet on Cicely Battishill——'

'Hold,' said Herring, angrily; 'I dare you——'

'I will not be stayed. You pitied the girl; you were constantly with her, you were tender and foolish. I do not dispute your good taste. White and roses, and auburn hair—a young fellow might do worse than pick up with Cicely. Well, for her sake you sold some of the stones, and bought up the mortgages on West Wyke, held by my father. Was that fair? My father had refused to invest Mirelle's money in that, and you took her money unknown to him and thus employed it—only for the sake of pretty Cicely.'

'I will not suffer such words to be spoken,' said Herring; 'I have never regarded Miss Battishill in any other light than that of a sister.'

'A very affectionate brother you have been! So very fond of this dear pink-and-white sister that you desert your wife and spend all your time with her. You ran away the day after your marriage, and have not shown your face to your wife since till this day, and now you are off again, allured back to West Wyke by the superior attractions of Cicely Battishill.'

Herring's blood boiled up, and he struck Sampson in the face between the eyes, and sent him staggering back against the wall.

'Dare to say another such word again!'

'I will dare,' answered Sampson, when he had gathered himself together. He quivered with rage. 'I will dare, because it is true. Are you not going back now to Cicely? You know you are.' How did he know this, Herring wondered. He had no idea that Sampson had possessed himself of the address left in the bureau.

'Who bought his wife with her own money, eh?' pursued the enraged Sampson. 'Cobbledick told me once of a man who bought a wife in Okehampton market for a crown. You have bought Mirelle. That man paid a crown for her out of his own pocket; but you, you picked Mirelle's pocket for the purchase money. Is not this true? Was ever a more dastardly act done than that? You called me a scoundrel. I may not have always acted on the square, but, by God, I never did such a crooked job as this. Did you know that Mirelle was over head and ears in love with Captain Trecarrel? Of course you did. You knew that well enough, and, lest he should marry her, you kept from her the secret of her wealth. You let her and the Captain suppose they were too poor to marry, and so he was ready to sell himself to Orange for five thousand pounds, when in heart he was tied to Mirelle. Was that honourable—was that gentlemanly—was that honest? Eh! Answer me that. No, no, my friend, virtuous John. You were too clever. You wanted to steal the fortune and wipe the guilt off your conscience, and so you marry Mirelle whilst spooning that other one. But how do you manage this? Mirelle don't care a snap of the fingers for you. When the failure of Ophir brought ruin on my family you allowed my lady to feel the misery of beggary, and then you came to the rescue and overwhelmed her with your generosity—mind you, generous you were with her money. You relieved her necessities out of her own purse, and never let her suspect it, in the hopes of rousing in her the feeling of gratitude to her great-hearted protector. What could the poor girl do but accept you as a husband? She could not live on your alms; that would not be decent, would it? A lady cannot receive four hundred a year and a house from a young officer and preserve her character. She must marry him, or relinquish what he has given her, and that latter alternative she cannot take without involving Orange and my mother in poverty. Thus it was that you drove Mirelle to accept you. A very ingeniously contrived plan, certainly. Look how all the parts hang together, very perfect, and faulty only in this, that I was not consulted. A very ingenious plan, but cursedly wicked. By God! Even I would have shrunk from so dirty and scoundrelly a trick, and I am not squeamish. Give me some money.'

Herring held out his purse—a steel purse of interwoven links, with steel clasp, a present from Mirelle. His head had fallen on his breast; he was broken with shame and humiliation. This that Sampson had said was true, but Herring had never seen his conduct in the light that Sampson turned on it. It had never occurred to him that Mirelle could not accept his bounty without accepting him—that he had, as Sampson had said, driven her to take him, using her necessities as the whip, and that he had in fact bought her with her own money. He saw this now vividly, and the sight overcame him. He had been led by his conscience into conduct unworthy of a man of honour; he was degraded in his own eyes. Sampson took the purse, counted the money in his hand, returned it to the purse, snapped it, and slipped it into his pocket.

'That will do for a time. Well! you called me a scoundrel. Which is the biggest scoundrel of the two, Blackguard Sampson or Virtuous John? You regard my father as a robber of orphans; which robbed the orphan most? My father lost her six thousand pounds, you plundered her of more than twice that amount, and with it you carried off her happiness. Faugh! Virtuous John! even I turn away in disgust from you. I stand white and shining as an angel beside you. Nor is this all. No sooner is Mirelle yours and you can conscientiously keep her money, than you break her heart by deserting her for another girl with more pink in her cheeks than my Lady White Lily.'

Herring looked up; he was deadly pale, and his lips trembled. 'This is false.'

'What! is it false that you left Mirelle directly you had brought her hither?' Sampson waited for an answer. There could be none. It was true.

'Is it false that you returned at once to West Wyke?' He waited again. It was true, Herring had returned.

'Did you inform your wife whither you were going?' Silence again. Herring had not told her; he had declined to do so.

'No, you evaded telling her. You went back to West Wyke—to Cicely the rosebud, and you have been with her—your pretty pink-and-white sister— ever since. How kind to Mirelle to rescue her rival from ruin with her money! You think Mirelle will appreciate this when told. And told the whole story of your dealings she shall be this very night.'

'Have done,' said Herring, in a low tone. 'Leave me alone.'

'No, not yet,' answered Sampson, triumphantly. 'You have insulted and injured me, and I shall not leave you till I have made you sting and writhe. You robbed Mirelle of that which ought to have been put into the hands of my father and me, her diamonds; that is offence number one. You insulted me at West Wyke, and threatened me with a ruler; that was offence number two. I took a fancy to Mirelle, and might have contrived to win her and her money, but you stood in the way by retaining her diamonds, and with them you kept a hold over her destiny; that was offence number three. You exposed Ophir— you brought that pretty and flourishing affair to an end before it was ripe; that was a bad offence, number four. To you I owe the vagabond life I have been living ever since, number five; and to you a blow just now received, to make up the number to six. Shall not I repay these when I may? Do you not know that now my father is dead I step into his position as trustee of Mirelle's fortune, till she is three-and-twenty? There is no provision in the will relative to marriage. If you, curse you, had not brought the dogs of justice out of kennel and set them after me, I would claim the diamonds of you, and exact every penny you have spent. I cannot do it now, situated as I am. You have hunted me down for that very reason—you dreaded me, lest I should find out your fraud as you found out mine; you forestalled me, and now you drive me out of England to prevent me from reclaiming from you what you have no right to retain. You are very clever; I never gave you credit for half your talent. But for all your cleverness, you shall not escape. You think that your wife need know nothing of what has taken place. She shall know everything. Do you remember a confession you wrote to her? Well, I took it from the drawer where you had hidden it, and I have given it into her hands. That was the first mouthful, she shall receive next my commentary on it.'

'What!' exclaimed Herring, white, trembling, the sweat standing in beads on his brow.

'Ah! you may well be scared at the thought. That trustful Mirelle, who believed in you as the most honourable of men, has learned this night what you are—a despicable thief. She has discovered what you really are, and how you circumvented her, and robbed her of her liberty, and forged out of her own gold the chain that binds her to you. She knows now the man she has married—and from this night forward she loathes him.'

Herring could not speak; his heart stood still.

'She is now, I doubt not, pacing her bedroom, cursing that man whom she once respected, but whom she now knows to be dishonest, untruthful, and treacherous, the man who has blighted her entire life.'

Then Sampson laughed at the poor, paralysed, broken wretch before him, eyed him from head to foot, turned his back, and with his one hand in a pocket, and the other swinging his bundle of old clothes, he left the office.

Without was night, black and starless.

'I have given him a worse blow than he gave me, I guess,' said Sampson; 'now all I have to do is to dispose of this bundle and then make off to Falmouth as fast as I can. By heavens, I wish the night had not fallen so dark, I cannot make out whither I am going. I can hear the sea, and when I reach the edge I shall see the foam, and then over goes the bundle. It makes me laugh to think how John Herring looked. I might have been stabbing him all the time with a little knife; but, faith, I reckon my words went deeper than knives. I wish it were not so confoundedly dark. Curse it!—where am I?'

Where?

Below was Blackapit, with the waves leaping in that cauldron of darkness.

One minute more and the leaping waters were flinging Sampson Tramplara from side to side, and the gulls were flapping their wings and screaming applause over a bruised and lifeless body.

CHAPTER LVI.

A DEAD MAN.

Herring was back at West Wyke. Everything went on there as usual. The mine was worked systematically. The absence of John Herring for a few days mattered little. West Wyke never altered. Since it had been built, no Squire had added a room or an outhouse. But from year to year it ripened and mellowed, the lichens spread over the stones in wider patches of orange and white, and the stones became more wrinkled, and the ribs of the roof more prominent through the slopes of small slate.

Cicely was the same—sweet, sunny, simple. Herring thought that nowhere in the wide world could a more restful spot be found than this, or more soothing society. Cicely saw that he looked more broken after this last visit to Welltown than after the former. What was the mystery that hung over his life—what the grief that consumed his heart? His former visit had transformed him from a youth to a man, but this had aged him almost to decrepitude. Cicely observed this, but she said nothing. She troubled him with no inquiries, she did not even allow him to perceive that she noticed a change. The change was not so much in his exterior as within. A cleavage had gone down into his moral nature. On the former occasion his hopes had been shattered, now his faith was shaken. Before he had been broken-hearted, now he was broken-spirited. His interview with Sampson had shaken his confidence in himself, he could no longer rely on conscience as a safe guide, and he knew of no other prompter to action. He reviewed his course of conduct again and again, and always came to the same conclusion, that he was justified in what he had done. What was the alternative course—the course from which conscience had turned him? That was to have given up the box to Trampleasure and washed his hands of all responsibility. But that would have been selfish conduct; it would have been cruel as it was heartless. No doubt he had been influenced by his love for Mirelle when he concealed his discovery from the legal trustee, but he would have done the same for any other helpless person similarly situated, knowing as he did that to betray the secret was to ruin the ward. And to what had he been led? To the wrecking of two lives, of his own and that of Mirelle. If he had acted according to legal instead of moral right, this would not, perhaps, have taken place. How is a man to govern his life—what is to be the mainspring of his actions? The statute law, or the law of God written in the heart? Herring had lost faith in the guidance of conscience, in the directing hand of Providence. He remembered the words of Mirelle on the walk to Welltown, 'All the familiar landmarks fail me, all the ways lead in unknown directions, I am translated into a country that I am expected to travel through without a map or guide.' Those words, which were void of meaning to him when spoken, precisely described his present condition. The framework of his moral consciousness was shaken and out of joint. In time, perhaps, he would recover, but at present the shock had thrown him out of his perpendicular. In Japan, the land of earthquakes, every tower is held upright and together by a huge pendulum of beamwork hanging free. The moral conscience is the pendulum in man. When that is strapped and braced to the girders and buttresses without, a little shock throws the whole system into ruin. It must hang free if it is to serve as a source of stability, otherwise it precipitates ruin. The human heart can endure any amount of disappointment so long as it maintains its faith in the eternal Providence, but, when that fails, its powers of endurance are at an end. Then the wave of bitterness rises and washes over the soul and leaves it like the Desert of Nitre, strewn with bones. The dew of heaven may drop, the showers may fall on it, but the white, bitter surface thenceforth can never laugh into verdure.

John Herring did his work mechanically. He took neither pleasure nor interest in it. The mine might prosper, it probably would, and the result would be evil. He would clear the estate of Cicely from its encumbrances. What for? —good; nothing led to good—to find that he had done mischief in his effort to help her. Everywhere men and women are striving to amend wrongs, and only succeed in shifting the suffering from the shoulders of one class on to another. Everywhere dirty pools are being scraped out, only to discolour and defile the water that is disturbed. Everywhere tortured humanity is being inoculated with matter that will expel one disease by preparing the soil for another.

'Please, miss,' said Joyce, one Sunday, to Cicely, who had just returned from church, 'there be that fool of a Jim White from Coombow have a come all the way, and what he be come for I don't know.'

'What Jim White?'

'A buffleheaded sort of a chap,' said Joyce, in a tone between shyness and disgust; 'he it were as brought me and the master here that day as he were nigh upon killed by Sampson Tramplara.'

Herring looked up; he was at the table. He had not been to church; why should he go to church to be bidden follow conscience when conscience leads astray? Why should he seek for light when the only light afforded is that of Jack o'lanthorns that lead into mires? He said bitterly, 'Joyce, why did you bring me hither?'

'I couldn't do nort other—I did it to make you well again.'

She had followed her conscience, and her poor light had led her to save his life. What for?—to make Mirelle miserable and himself miserable. Better a thousand times had he died then.

'But, Joyce, what about Jim White? What does he want?'

'Well, miss, I dunnow exactly what he wants, but he've a walked all these miles, and he've a got to go back again, so what I want to know is, may he have his meat here, as he ain't a going to get nort else?'

'Certainly.'

'And he may have a drop o' cyder to his meat? Jim White be one as can't get on without that. And he smells o' cyder now like as old vaither's cask did when it were fresh.'

'By all means, Joyce,' said Cicely, 'and you may invite him to come here once a month.'

Joyce flushed up. 'I—I don't want the bufflehead to be coming here. I've a told 'n so scores and scores o' times, and I'll tell him if he comes again he'll get neither meat nor cyder. He were here about a month ago, I reckon, and he sed he'd that partikler to say as could only be said between four eyes. So he sat in the kitchen on one chair, and I on another, a full two hours by the clock, and he never opened his mouth all that time but once, to ax why the great beam went across the ceiling. There! he shall have his meat this Sunday, and, by the blue blazes, he shan't have it of me no more.' Then she stepped up to Herring. 'Please, maister,' she said, 'Jim White have a brought you a paper from Okehampton, a "Saturday News"; he sez he thought you'd a like to see 'n. I didn't think the chap had it in 'n.'

'Thank you, Joyce, and thank Jim White, and here is a present to him for his mistaken kindness to me on a former occasion.'

'But,' said Joyce, 'I may tell 'n that you don't want the paper again. He be that stupid he might make the bringing of a paper an excuse to come here every Sunday. I know,' she exclaimed brightly—'I know what I'll do. I'll tell 'n if he comes again you'll up with your gun and bang off wi' it as you did at me to Welltown that night.'

'Very well; as you like.'

When Joyce had retired, Herring took up the paper indifferently. It could not interest him, for nothing interested him now.

'I wish you had been at church to-day, John,' said Cicely; 'Mr. Harmless-Simpleton preached us a very good sermon.'

'Indeed—on what text?' asked John Herring, carelessly.

'After death, the judgment.'

Herring laughed bitterly. 'Cicely,' he said, 'the order is inverted. The judgment comes first, and after that—after a long and weary interval—death. At least that is my experience.'

She looked at him with a distressed and puzzled expression. 'Dear Cousin John, what has come over you? you are so different from what you were.'

'What has come over me?' he echoed; 'the judgment and condemnation. There! ask no more questions. Take the paper and look at it; there is nothing in it to interest me.' He pushed it across the table to her.

'Do you take no interest in politics, John?'

'No; they are only Ophir over again.'

'John, I cannot understand you. Why are you so changed in your view of life? At one time you were hopeful and believed in good, and now you despair and believe only in evil. You make me unhappy.'

'Then I am fulfilling my destiny. The curse is laid on me to blight all I come across.'

'That is utterly untrue.'

'We see life in different lights, Cicely. In after years you will recognise that my view is the true view. Fortunately, the young who start in life are nursed in delusions, or they would refuse the race.'

'John,' said Cicely, 'what is the meaning of this?' She had been turning listlessly over the paper, listening to Herring's words, and troubled in her mind about him. 'Here stands your name—and Welltown, your place in Cornwall.'

'What!' he asked; 'let me look.' And he took the paper hastily out of her hands.

He read of the discovery of Mr. John Herring, late of Welltown, who had disappeared from home on a certain night, but without any suspicions having been raised till his body was found in Plackapit at low water a few days later, terribly mangled and defaced. It would not have been possible to identify the body but for the clothes worn by the deceased, and which had been taken from the place in his office where they usually hung. Moreover, the pocket contained a steel purse known to have belonged to the deceased gentleman, and in the breast-pocket was discovered a magnificent set of diamonds, the property of his wife, which she always kept in a concealed drawer, the secret of which was known only to herself and Mr. Herring. According to what had transpired, the last time the deceased was seen alive was by his wife, seated at the bureau in which these diamonds were. Apparently he had removed the jewels before leaving; for what purpose it was impossible to conjecture, especially as it was suspected that the deceased gentleman had committed suicide. It was reported that he had written a farewell letter to his wife at the bureau where she saw him, intimating his intention; but this letter she absolutely refused to produce at the inquest. This melancholy event had cast a deep gloom over the entire neighbourhood, &c. &c.

Herring read this paragraph over twice before he could understand it, and even then he understood it only imperfectly. But the main points flashed out. Sampson Tramplara had fallen over the rocks, and his body had been mistaken for that of himself because of the clothes he wore and the purse in his pocket. How Sampson had obtained the diamonds he was unable to divine, but he suspected that the letter alluded to was that containing his confession, which Sampson had told him he had given to Mirelle. He sat looking mutely at the paper, his mind working.

'What is it, John?' asked Cicely; but he did not hear. Then she came to him and looked over his shoulder.

'John,' said she, putting her hand on him and shaking him; 'John, what is the meaning of this?'

'Cicely, it is as I said—after judgment, death. Do you see? I am a dead man.'

There was silence in the room. She was collecting her thoughts. What did this all mean?

'John,' she exclaimed, 'what is this?—you have a wife!'

'No—a widow.'

Then he stood up, and walked twice up and down the room, his face white as ashes, his hands behind his back, and his head bowed. Cicely followed him with her eyes; she was bewildered.

'It is best as it is,' said he to himself. 'Mirelle is set free. John Herring is dead.'

Then the truth rushed in on Cicely's mind.

'Oh, John, John! Was she—Mirelle, your wife?'

He looked at her. He did not answer; she saw the mute agony in his face.

'Oh, John, poor John! now I understand all! Now I know why you have been so unhappy. I am sure she never loved you.'

'No, Cicely, she never loved me.'

'She could love no one.'

'You are wrong; she loved another.'

139

Again there was silence. Cicely's eyes filled.

Herring paced the room again. Cicely could not see him now, her eyes were too full.

'Oh, John! dear, poor John!'

'Cicely,' he said, standing still in the midst of his tramp, 'what has happened is best for every one. Let it be. From henceforth John Herring is dead. If you will, I am John Battishill, your brother.'

CHAPTER LVII.

AN ARREST.

A blustering day; the rain splashing against the windows of an inn at Plymouth. Mirelle sat in the window; there was a balcony with balustrade before it, and the water dripped incessantly from the rail upon the swimming balcony.

Mirelle was in mourning; her face looked preternaturally white in her black dress. Her eyes were sunken, her lips thin and tremulous; but there were spots of almost colour in her cheeks, speaking of feverish excitement, not of health. Genefer Benoke was with her.

'Mistress,' said the old woman, 'be it still too late to bid you turn back? I tell'y I don't believe as the master be dead. I don't believe it, though I saw him dead with my own eyes. For the eyes of the understanding be keener and clearer than they of the flesh. When Saul the persecutor were cast to the ground on his way to Damascus, he opened his eyes and saw no man. That be the state of most. They've their eyes open, but they sees naught that they ought to see. They goes through the world and they don't see the snares that be set on every side, and the angels that compass them about, and the Providence as is leading of them. The eyes of the flesh be open, but the eyes of the understanding see nothing. With the eyes of the soul I see the master still alive. Afore you came to Welltown I saw you; and I saw what was to be, in a vision, and whether I were in the body or out of the body at the time I cannot tell—God knoweth; but this I do say, that what I then saw with the spiritual eye don't accord no ways with what the natural eye declares. But what do I speak of this to you for as if you knowed naught about the spiritual eye? Sure alive, you lead a life of prayer as do I. Well, I will tell'y what were revealed to me. I fell into a trance, having my eyes open, and I saw the master with his arms round you—the Bride of Snow—and he looked up to you, seeking in you that he never saw.'

Mirelle bowed her face in her hands.

'And with the warmth of his heart you melted away, drop by drop. I've a seen how you've a been thawing right away ever since the day he brought you to Welltown, tear by tear—as see! you be melting now. And in my vision I saw that you dissolved clean away and your place knew you no more; but nevertheless the master remained, with his arms extended and his eyes uplifted, as though still seeking you, till he grew cold, and his hair white, and his tears ice, and his heart were frozen dead. You was gone first, and, after a space, he; it be against the truth of my vision that he should die first and you after.'

'Geneviève, there can be no doubt whatever about what has happened. I would cheerfully give my life to restore his, but that cannot be. I know for certain that he is dead. I have many and weighty reasons for so believing.'

'What reasons? It be true enough that your diamonds and the purse were found on him, as well as his own old clothes that I've a sewed the brass buttons on—I know them well. But what about that? The devil be crafty, and given power to deceive.'

'I have other reasons.'

'I ask you what? You may tell me, for we shall never meet in the flesh again.'

'He wrote to me the night he died. He had been talking to me in my boudoir, and was very unhappy. Then he told me he would write me something, and I gave him the key of my cabinet, where were my diamonds and my writing materials. When I opened the desk next morning the jewels were gone, and I found his letter. In that letter he told me that he bade me farewell for ever.

'He meant to go abroad.'

'No, Geneviève, the letter said more than that. It intimated that, when I received it, I should be——'

'What?'

'What I now am—a widow.'

'It be a temptation of the devil,' said Genefer, 'who is mighty to deceive, who be come down with great wrath for that he hath a short time. You never let no one see the letter?'

'No. Unfortunately I spoke of it to Orange, and that is how anything come out about it. I thought she would have been more discreet.'

'Well, well!' sighed Genefer; 'the world be full of delusions. Now you be going back to France and to wicked idolatry. There be no call of God in that, to leave the land of light for that of darkness.'

'Geneviève, do not speak on this subject. You and I cannot see alike. I am seeking rest, I am weary, utterly weary of the life I have led in England. It is useless your attempting to argue with me, and to dissuade me from it. I am weary of the wind and the clouds and the rain and the roar of waves without, and of the troubles that toss and overcast the soul within. I must go back. I must find peace. I count the hours till I am within those blessed happy doors of the Sacré Coeur again; and, when once within, I will never, never, never leave that home. Come, Geneviève, help me on with my cloak and hood. I mast go out; the rain has ceased, and I will see if there be a chance of the storm abating.'

'Mistress, the packet won't sail with a gale on shore such as this. It would be tempting of Providence.'

'You will come with me. I am impatient of the delay. I must see what the sky and sea look like, and you must attend me, as I cannot stand unassisted against the force of the wind. Oh, Geneviève! where I am going I shall feel no storms—I shall be in perfect shelter, and at rest.'

Mirelle was, as she said, on her way to France. From the time that she knew she was free, one absorbing desire had taken hold of her—the desire to fly from England and return to the convent of the Sacred Heart, there to bury herself from the world. The world, against which the sisters had warned her, she had seen. It was full of unrest, brutality, self-seeking, and imposture. She thought all day of her escape, she dreamt of her return all night. So completely had this idea taken hold of her that it excluded all other thoughts; it possessed her like a fever. She could not think of John Herring. Even Captain Trecarrel was far from her mind. She wanted nothing for the future but perfect quiet within the sacred walls of the Sacré Coeur.

Those of old who were accused of witchcraft were kept without sleep till they confessed. They were denied a moment's doze, till, in the craving for rest, they admitted whatever they were charged with, ready to face the flames if only they might first fold their hands and close their eyes and sigh away their spirits into oblivion.

Some such a craving had come over Mirelle. She had been denied the rest she desired, she had been distracted by responsibilities she did not understand, buffeted by rude associates, placed in situations full of bewilderment, deprived of the ministrations of religion, and, now that the possibility of escape opened to her, she became almost mad to seize it.

Mirelle had told her intention to Orange, who warmly approved of it, and Orange and Genefer had accompanied her to Plymouth, where she wras to take passage to France. They had spent a night on the way at Dolbeare, and Genefer was to return with Orange the day after Mirelle had departed.

An arrangement had been proposed by Orange, and readily acquiesced in by Mirelle, that Mrs. Trampleasure and Orange were to remain at Welltown, at least for a while, and take charge of the estate; they were to retain a certain portion of the receipts, and forward the rest to Mirelle.

Mirelle was to have sailed on the day when we have reintroduced her to the reader, seated in the inn window at Plymouth, but the storm had prevented the packet from sailing. Her passage was paid, her berth taken, and her luggage was on board. If the weather abated, she would leave England for ever on the morrow.

Attended by Genefer Benoke, Mirelle went out upon the Hoe and looked forth on the noble bay. There was then no breakwater across its entrance, arresting the violence of the swell. The waves, driven by a south-westerly gale, rolled in from the sea and foamed about the headlands that jutted into the harbour. They tossed and danced about Drake Island and Mount Batten, and ran hissing upon the white marble shore beneath the Hoe. The rain had abated, but fresh showers were coming on, stalking over the angry sea and staining it to ink beneath them. There was no sign of a cessation in the gale. It came on in furious gusts, before which Mirelle cowered and clung to Genefer. As she turned on one occasion, a gentleman standing near, also observing the sea, saw her face, and uttered an exclamation of surprise. She raised her eyes and met those of Captain Trecarrel.

'Mirelle!' he exclaimed, and hastened to interpose his umbrella between her and the wind. 'How unexpected! What brings you to Plymouth? It is my fate to light on you where least anticipated. I have completed my excursion and filled my portfolio. I returned by the south coast to see whether it furnished material for a second issue of pictures, and here I am at Plymouth meditating a return to Launceston as soon as the weather clears. I was so shocked to hear of your loss. I always respected John Herring as a worthy, well-meaning man. There was no pretence about him, no affectation of being other than he was. I have no doubt that his death was an awful blow to you— so sudden, and the manner so dreadful. You have my warmest sympathy. Poor fellow! poor fellow! Well, well, the world is short of a good sterling man it could ill afford to lose. I hope his circumstances were all right, no money trouble?'

Mirelle shook her head.

'You do not think that distress about over-expenditure can have affected his brain? Inability to meet calls?'

145

'He was well off—rich—much richer than I thought,' said Mirelle, sadly. 'But pray, Captain, spare me now.'

'Allow me your arm,' said Trecarrel; 'the wind is so high that I am in momentary fear of your being blown off the cliff and being carried out to sea.'

'The wind is on shore,' said Mirelle, drily.

'True, true; I had not observed it. Bah! here comes the rain, driving as you say on shore, and irresistible. Under these circumstances there is no cowardice in beating a retreat and evacuating the Hoe to the enemy. Shall we descend? Where are you staying? At the Royal? Let me accompany you home. What! Genefer Benoke here? How do you do, Genefer? Sad time you have had at Welltown. My heart has bled for you all. I would have flown to the spot to offer my services, but some sorrows are too sacred to be intruded on. I never was more shocked in my life than when I heard of the accident, if accident it may be called, but I suppose it really was that, if he was unembarrassed in circumstances.' So talking, asking questions and getting no answers, Captain Trecarrel accompanied Mirelle back to the inn. He did not wait to be invited to enter, but accompanied Mirelle upstairs.

'Now tell me all about it,' he said. 'I would not return to Welltown after the sad event, through delicacy of sentiment; I thought it might augment your trouble. So I continued my sketching tour, and really made some capital drawings. The weather, however, proved detestable, and after a while I gave up the north coast and took a flying survey of the south. And now, tell me why you are here. What can have brought you to Plymouth?'

'Captain Trecarrel, I am on my way to France, to the convent of the Sacré Coeur, where I was educated.'

'Nothing of the sort. You are going to stay in England.'

Mirelle shook her head. 'No; my mind is made up. Indeed, from the moment that I knew my husband was dead, and that I was a free agent, I had no doubt as to what I must do.'

'You are not dreaming of shutting yourself up in a convent?'

'I am going home.'

'Home! what do you mean by home?'

'I mean whatever you associate with rest and fragrance and holiness, with love and innocence and happiness. Some find this ideal in a family. I have never had any experience of home in this sense; the only family I have been with was that of the Trampleasures, and that in no way comes up to my ideal. I will not say more about that. No! what I mean by home is that which I know—the convent of the Sacré Coeur.'

Trecarrel rubbed his chin musingly, and then pulled his moustache. 'If you become a nun, what is to become of Welltown? You are, I presume, well off. Herring had no brothers and sisters, and that falls to you I suppose. Are you thinking of selling John Herring's property, of calling in all your available funds, and bestowing everything on the convent and the bears of Paris?'

'I have not this thought. Orange and her mother will reside at Welltown and manage the estate, and let me have the money I need.'

'And who will check their accounts—who look after your interests?'

'Orange will send me what I want. I do not require much.'

'What did my poor friend John Herring die worth? That is—how much has come to you, Mirelle?'

'I do not know the value of the Welltown estate.'

'But I do,' said Trecarrel, sharply. 'Six hundred nett, on the outside. Is that all?'

'No,' answered Mirelle, 'there is a great deal more money than that. Many thousand pounds. There are the mortgages on West Wyke, and there is a mine somewhere about there, and money beside.'

'All yours?' asked Trecarrel, turning his melting blue eye on Mirelle, and stroking his moustache.

'I suppose so.'

'And this is all to be left to the unchecked management of Orange?'

'Yes, Orange is so kind and sensible, she will know better than I what ought to be done, and how to do it.'

'Mirelle!' exclaimed the Captain, standing up, and placing himself before the fire, occupying the entire rug; 'you are not going to leave England. You are not going to shirk your duty.'

'My duty! I have done that to the best of my powers, which are small. No, Captain Trecarrel, I must go back whence I came. You cannot conceive how abhorrent to me has been the life I have led since I came to England. It has nearly killed me. Look at my hands; they were plump when I left France, compared to what they are now. My strength is gone; a very short walk now tires me out. I was strong before. I have had no illness whatever except that fever at Dolbeare before I was married, but my soul has been sick ever since I left France, and now I feel a sort of instinct in me that if I am to live I must spread my wings and escape over the water to dear France and nestle into the old convent home again.'

'No, Mirelle, you would not find rest there, you may take my word for it. You would carry thither something in your heart which would forbid your finding rest there. Look me in the face and say that this is not so.' She could not do this; there was truth in his words. 'No, dear Mirelle, that old convent life is no more to be returned to than childhood. You may, as an adult, go back into the nursery, and buy a rattle and feed yourself with pap out of a spoon; but you cannot revive the old childish buoyancy of heart and brightness of hope, you go back into infantine surroundings with the care-furrowed heart of age. You would not be happy in the convent, because you return to it a woman and you went out a child. There is something more to be considered; you have contracted obligations which you have no right to cast off. You own an estate and a fortune, and this gives you influence and power for good; this you have no right to ignore. You have been transplanted by Providence to a place where religion is as dead or diseased as when Saint Morwenna came to the same coast twelve hundred years ago. Do you suppose she came to it by choice? Do you think that she never yearned to be back in the stillness and indolence of her dear convent at Burton? She came to our Cornish coast from a sunny home in the midlands, among lime-trees and buttercup pastures, and from a church where there was sweet music and rich sculpture and all the splendours of Catholic worship, and inhabited a rude hovel overhanging the sea, into which the storm drove between the ill-jointed stones; away from trees and flowers, and music and worship, simply and solely because she was called to live there, and duty tied her to the spot. Now we venerate Saint Morwenna as a Virgin Apostle of the Cornish Coast, as one who brought light to those in darkness, the truth to those in error. You are a Catholic. Was it any choice of yours which took you to Welltown? You were taken there by Providence, and Providence has set you a task which you have no right to leave undone, has given you a post which you dare not desert. Those poor wretched Cornish are like shipwrecked men lost in night and storm, not knowing whither to steer, and led astray by wreckers' lanthorns. You are sent among them as a second Morwenna, to lead them to the true port, to show them the only true light.'

'I—I—I!' Mirelle trembled, and her heart sank within her: she had not strength and courage to execute such a task.

'Yes, you. With your means and position you can do a great deal. Who is there at Boscastle to oppose you? Sir Jonathan? He will do nothing. How do you know but that you may win his daughters, and so save their souls? Who is there of influence for miles round except yourself and the Phyllacks? Build a Catholic Chapel at Boscastle, down in the midst of the people. Establish there a priest and a mission, and every soul brought into the true fold will bless you.'

Mirelle was silent.

'I am pointing out to you a duty. You have seen no priest since you were married; you must suffer me to be your director. Has not what I urge struck you before?'

'No,' answered Micelle, faintly. 'But see! I can do much that you say, and yet live in France. I will endow a mission at Boscastle and build there a church.'

'You cannot set a missioner there without a soul to support him. He must have one or two Catholics near, or he can do nothing. Now you understand what I said. If you fly abroad you take trouble along with you, and you will not rest in your convent. It is the story of Jonah over again, and see—see this storm sent to arrest you, to send you back to Nineveh, from which you were flying.'

'How cruel you are—how cruel! I have been so hoping, longing, sighing to escape.'

Cruel indeed he was, and mean beneath conception. He used the words and arguments which he knew would tell with her, not that he cared for the souls of the Boscastle people, or for the advance of the Catholic Church, but because he coveted her money and the estate of Welltown.

'That is not all,' continued Captain Trecarrel, and his tone changed from that of exhortation to that of pleading. His voice melted, and sounded as though tears were welling up in it; it became soft and tremulous. 'You have no right to run away, dear Mirelle, for another reason. You know—you know'—his voice became broken; then, with a gulp, swallowing his agitation —'you know what I mean.'

Mirelle trembled. She did know what he meant.

'You have no right to sacrifice another as well as yourself. You know, Mirelle, how I have loved you—'

'Stay, stay!' exclaimed Mirelle, piteously. 'Do not speak to me again like this. I must—I must go. If only to pray for my poor husband's soul, I must go.'

'Mirelle, tell me—do you believe that he wilfully destroyed himself?'

'I do.'

'For what reason? There were no money troubles?'

'None whatever.'

'Why, then, did he commit suicide?'

She was silent. She could not explain. He considered for a while, and then said, 'How is it that there had been such an estrangement between you from the beginning? I understand he left you the day after the marriage, and did not return till that day which ended in his death. This is very mysterious, and points to some great cause of trouble between you. Did he love you?'

'Indeed he did. Too well.'

'Did you love him?'

She did not answer, but her head sank on her bosom.

'Tell me, Mirelle—is it true that he wrote to you the night of his death? I heard a report to that effect.'

'Yes, it is true.'

'What did he say in that letter?'

She hesitated. 'He said that he bade me farewell for ever. He said that when I read the letter I should be free.'

'Why did he write thus?'

She made no answer, but covered her face.

'Tell me, Mirelle—did he know of my—of our——'

'Spare me—spare me! Oh, Captain Trecarrel, if you must know all, he knew that I did not love him in the way in which he loved me, and the knowledge of this made him so miserable that—— You know the rest. And now, do you not see that I have his death on my conscience, and I must do what I can to expiate this sin, and do what I can for the poor despairing soul that I drove to despair?'

'Set your mind at ease. I do not in the least believe in his self-destruction. A man about to commit suicide does not first fill his pocket with diamonds worth several thousand pounds. The finding of the jewels upon him is conclusive evidence that he did not meditate self-destruction, but, on the contrary, meant to live comfortably on the proceeds of their sale elsewhere. John Herring—you may take my word for it—made up his mind, as he could not be happy with you, that he would go elsewhere, probably to America. Now, a man cannot start afresh in life penniless without great inconvenience and discomfort: so he laid his hand on that which was convertible into money, to start him in the New World. You do not suppose John Herring intended to strangle himself with a diamond necklace, do you? If he did not, the supposition of his having meditated self-destruction is untenable beside the fact of his having taken the jewels. No; he possessed himself of them because he had not sufficient cash in hand, and as he made his way over the cliffs—it was a dark night—he missed his path and fell down Blackapit. There you have the solution of the entire mystery. Set your mind at ease; the guilt of his death does not weigh on you, and there is no need for you to expiate it in a convent.'

Mirelle breathed more freely. This explanation did really seem the correct one, and the relief it gave her was great.

'Now, then,' said the Captain, 'I have knocked this nonsense of cloistering yourself on the head.' He rang the bell, and, when the servant appeared, he said, 'Send to the packet, and have the Countess Garcia's boxes brought back. She is not going to sail in her.'

Mirelle raised her hand in protest, but in vain. The strong will and determination of the Captain was more than she could resist in her present weak condition.

'Listen now to me, dear Mirelle,' he said, and, leaving the fire, came towards her. 'The barrier that has stood between us has fallen. What is there now to hinder you from becoming my wife? I have loved you from the first moment that I saw you, and—do not deny it—you have loved me. You

152

married a man for whom you did not care—a worthy man, but not one a heart like yours could cling to, even if disengaged; and disengaged it was not. Duty obliged you—obliged both of us—to smother and conceal our mutual love. But the fire was not extinguished, and, now that the obligation to keep it under exists no longer, it bursts forth in flame once more. You shall not go to France. If you do, in spite of me, I will follow you, and claim you from the sisters of the Sacred Heart. You have no right to run away; you owe me reparation for the suffering I have undergone. Shall I own to you something? I knew that you were going to sail in the packet; I knew what you purposed doing; and I came to Plymouth to prevent it.'

Mirelle looked up at him with surprise.

'Yes, dearest, when I knew that you were free I had no rest. I saw my hopes of happiness revive. Hender Benoke was in my pay. He kept me informed of what was taking place and what was meditated at Welltown. In love as in war, all things are lawful.'

Mirelle was now standing near the window, leaning against the angle of the window splay, with the curtain behind her. Her face was turned away. She could not look at the Captain, but she saw nothing through the window panes.

Captain Trecarrel came towards her. She felt his approach, she did not see it, and she trembled violently. She was powerless. The events of her short life in the world had broken down her force of character and power of resistance to a superior and resolute will.

'Mirelle, dearest Mirelle,' he said, in a voice vibrating with pathos, 'you said, a little while ago, that the only knowledge you had of home was a cloister; there is another and a fonder home—in the arms, on the heart, of a good and honourable man.' He put his arms round her and clasped her to him.

At the same moment the door opened, and Orange came in, very wet, with cheeks glowing with exercise; but when she saw the Captain holding Mirelle in his arms, and stooping to imprint a kiss on her lips, she turned the colour of parchment.

'Orange!' exclaimed the Captain, recovering himself at once. 'Delighted to see you. Mirelle is not going to France; she is not going to immure herself in a cloister; she returns to Launceston, and thence to Welltown to-morrow, and she has very kindly offered me a place in her carriage as far as Launceston. I do not in the least object to a seat with my back to the horses.'

CHAPTER LVIII.
R.I.P.

The chaise was ready to take Mirelle back again. She was depressed. A strange sinking, a sickening fear had come over her heart, the reaction after the excitement she had gone through, the eager expectation of a return to the convent, and then the arrest on the threshold of escape. She had painfully schooled herself not to think of the Captain, and even now she shrank from thinking of him, lest she should be committing a mortal sin. Even now, with the knowledge before her that he whom she had loved would claim her and be to her more than friend and support, she failed to feel anything but disappointment that she was not on her way back to the Sacré Coeur. She loved Trecarrel, but her love for him was not now the predominating feeling of her heart; her craving for rest and shelter prevailed over the other passion. Even now, if she could, she would have prosecuted her journey, and it was with a lingering, longing look that she gazed on the sea. Only duty, that supreme sense of submission to duty, drove her back. Captain Trecarrel knew her character perfectly when he appealed to this. The prospect of enjoying his love, of leaning on him, blunted the edge of her disappointment: it did no more than that.

Mirelle had not slept that night. Indeed she had not slept for several nights. Hitherto she had been kept awake by her fever of excitement at the prospect of return to the home of her childhood; last night she had been wakeful from other causes, disappointment, and bewilderment at the new landscape spread before her eyes. She looked like a girl convalescent from a long and dangerous sickness.

'Do you think, miss, her be fit to travel?' asked the hostess, compassionately, of Orange. 'Her looks a'most like death herself.'

'She suffers from the heart,' answered Orange, coldly.

Orange Trampleasure was not herself. A hard look had come over her face. The ripe, sensual lips were set and contracted, and a threatening light glimmered in her eyes.

'That other young lady do have a temper. I wouldn't be the one to cross her,' said the hostess to the chambermaid when the chaise departed.

Nor was Genefer herself the confident person she had been. Genefer was wont to speak as the oracle of the truth, to speak and act as though whatever she said and did was inspired. She had no doubt about her own infallibility, and every contrary opinion to hers she regarded as instigated by the devil. But this morning her confidence was gone; almost for the first time in her life she did not see her way clear before her. She had urged Mirelle to return to Welltown, and Mirelle was returning; but now Genefer doubted whether the advice she had given was wise and good. She did not like the Captain, and the Captain had succeeded in convincing her mistress when she had failed.

'The Lord have hid the thing from me!' she muttered as she mounted the box. She sat looking before her, waiting for the light, that she might see her way; but it did not come. At intervals she sighed, and muttered, 'I misdoubt me sore. But the Lord have closed my eyes that I cannot see.'

Strange as it may seem, the old woman had taken a strong liking for Mirelle, and it was not only because she thought Mirelle's object in returning to an idolatrous land was wrong that she opposed it, but also because in her rugged but warm heart she was attached to her and did not like to lose her. There was a singleness of mind and a spirituality of vision in the Snow Bride which impressed as well as puzzled Genefer. How one who was not a Dissenter could live an inner life, and pray much, perplexed her, but she recognised in Mirelle a good deal that was akin to herself, and she found that Mirelle entered into her spiritual experiences with interest and sympathy.

Orange sat by Mirelle, and Captain Trecarrel was opposite the latter. He made himself very agreeable, had a fund of conversation on a variety of topics, but found his companions in no responsive mood. He tried to interest Mirelle in the scenery, which was lovely, but Mirelle was absorbed in her thoughts and disinclined for conversation. The day was fine, the views looking back over Plymouth Bay and the woods of Mount Edgcumbe, the Hamoaze crowded with ships, and the winding estuary of the Tamar, were charming—hardly less beautiful were those in front, of Dartmoor. Mirelle leaned back in the chaise, the hood of which was thrown back, and the air fanned her face and soothed her.

Captain Trecarrel could hardly withdraw his eyes from her; she seemed to him the most lovely woman he had ever seen. He had an artist's appreciation of beauty of feature. The delicate and perfect chiselling of the nose and nostril, the finely formed, sensitive mouth, the pure brow, and, when she looked up, the solemn depth of her large eyes, filled him with admiration. A little lock of her dark hair had strayed over her forehead, and the soft warm air trifled with it in a tender, playful manner. Mirelle put up her fingers to put it in place, but unsuccessfully; it stole forth again, again to flutter in the light air.

Orange watched Trecarrel jealously; she saw how his eyes turned to Mirelle whenever he dare look at her without rudeness, and how his admiration of her beauty grew. The Captain spoke to her occasionally, but only by the way, his remarks were mainly directed to Mirelle, and when he turned to Orange she felt that he was doing so out of civility alone. His thoughts were not with her, but with her companion. Orange was not herself on this day; her usual colour had deserted her, and the sensuous fulness of life which throbbed in her seemed to have ebbed, and left her flaccid and pulseless.

Captain Trecarrel was aware that he had behaved badly to Orange, and had incurred her resentment; this made him nervous in her presence, and to hide his discomfort he redoubled his efforts to be agreeable. Finding that no conversation was to be got out of Mirelle, he finally turned his efforts to Orange, and endeavoured to amuse her with his adventures at the little inns on his sketching tour.

But still, as he talked, his eyes reverted to the face of Mirelle, and Orange's life returned in a throb of spleen. She rose in her seat and said sharply, 'We will change places, if you please, Captain Trecarrel.'

'Hush!' said he; 'do not disturb her. She sleeps.'

The fresh air puffing in her face, and the warm sun, after the sleepless nights, had operated on the weary brain, and Mirelle had dropped off into unconsciousness. Orange was aware of this without looking round, by the confidence with which the Captain allowed his eyes to rest on her face. Mirelle was breathing gently, and her face had become wonderfully peaceful and deathlike under the influence of sleep. The stray lock wantoned in the air on the pure white brow, but could not wake her.

'Do you really wish to sit with your back to the horses?' asked Trecarrel in an undertone. 'You will then have the sun in your eyes.'

'Yes, let us change places.' Her voice was metallic.

'Then, for the love of Heaven, do not wake her with moving. Stay! here we are at a long hill. I will get out and walk up it to relieve the horses, and then you can change without disturbing Mirelle.'

'If you are going to walk, I will walk also.'

They both alighted at the bridge over the Walkham, and fell behind the carriage. Trecarrel was uneasy; he feared that Orange was going to speak to him unpleasantly, on an unpleasant subject.

'She is so deficient in breeding,' said he to himself, 'that she persists in forcing herself and what she regards as her wrongs upon one.'

'How lovely she is!' exclaimed the Captain, with want of tact; 'but terribly fragile. She looks as if she were as likely never to wake out of the sleep into which she has fallen, as she is again to unclose her beautiful eyes.'

Orange made no answer. Her heart was beating; the rush of life had returned to her veins. She walked at his side in silence for some little way, then suddenly burst forth with, 'What is the meaning of this, Captain Trecarrel?'

'The meaning of what, my good Orange? You must be more explicit.'

'Why is Mirelle returning? How have you succeeded in changing her from her purpose? What inducement have you held out to her to lure her back to hated Welltown?'

'The highest, the purest of all,' answered the Captain, with dignity. 'For what is higher and purer than duty?'

Orange looked round at him.

'What do you mean by that?' she asked harshly. 'Duty—duty to whom?'

'To self—to conscience. I have pointed out to her obligations she must not cast off.'

'Duty—obligations!' echoed Orange, roughly. 'What farce is this? Have you turned preacher?'

'I have advised Mirelle as a friend. She has no one else capable of giving her counsel.'

'Indeed! I am nothing!'

'I beg your pardon, Orange. I do not ignore your high qualifications for advising her as to her social duties; but when we step out on moral ground, there I must beg leave to observe that only one of her own faith is calculated to direct her.'

Orange stood still and stamped her foot. Her hands clenched

convulsively.

'Captain Trecarrel! do you suppose me such a fool as to believe you when you take up this tone? I know you too well. I have suffered too severely from your selfishness and cruelty not to know that you are working in your own interest, disregarding everything and every one save some mean and selfish aim. Captain Trecarrel, you were bound to me by the most sacred vows, short of those made at the altar; you took a base advantage of my misfortunes to shake me off, when a man of honour and chivalry would have blushed to desert me. I humbled myself before you into the dust. I am covered with shame at the thought of such self-abasement before one so unworthy. You were without feeling for me, without love, without compassion, without generosity. After that you sought me again, when I had fled from Launceston to conquer my own heart in seclusion. You sought me out, you followed me to my place of retreat, to trifle with me again, to waken up in me what was going to sleep, to torture me, and to sting me to madness. Take care! take care! What have I done to you, that you should do this great wrong to me? I was a good-hearted and gay girl, without gall and bitterness, and you have turned my heart into a cauldron boiling with furious and hateful passions. Take care, I say; take care lest you drive me to desperation.'

'My dear, dear Orange——'

'Have done with "my dear, dear Orange!"' she almost shouted. The anger was boiling in her heart and puffing out the veins in her throat and temples. 'I am "dear" to you no more. Captain Trecarrel, you have had no mercy on me, and I appeal no more to you to consider my wrongs; but I do appeal to you on behalf of Mirelle, whom you so greatly admire, whom you profess to consider so lovely, whom you are guiding in the way of moral obligation. Have you no pity? Do you know to what you are driving her back? Can you not let her alone and allow her to escape whilst she may? Her heart is set on return to France and to her convent. Why should she not follow her heart and go? Why should you stand in the way, and lay your hand on her and arrest her? Let her go. It is not now too late. Let her follow her own wishes

159

and leave England. Do you not see that, tossed as she has been into a turmoil of troubles, they are killing her? It is a whirlpool sucking her in and suffocating her. Do not you incur the guilt of her destruction, as well as mine, you moral instructor! You have ruined my happiness, and with it my moral sense. You are thrusting her back out of happiness into death. She has been like a captive escaping from a dungeon, catching a glimpse of sun and laughing for joy, and now you, as a savage gaoler, come and drive her back into the rayless vault again, and cast a stone over the door. Cruel! cruel man!' She panted for breath. 'See,' she continued, 'see how fine the day is! The packet is now at sea with her prow turned towards France. But for your interference Mirelle would be on board, she would be standing on deck looking eagerly forward to catch the first sight of the loved land, her heart beating high with hope, her eye bright with returning happiness, her cheek flushed with renovated life. Let her go back to Plymouth and take the next packet.'

Captain Trecarrel said nothing, but, drawing a silk handkerchief from his pocket, he dusted his boots and faintly hummed a tune.

Orange's passion increased at his insulting indifference.

'Captain Trecarrel,' she said, 'have you no regard for any one but yourself? You think, do you, that some day Mirelle will be yours, and with her all she has?'

'Orange,' said the Captain, coldly, 'as you pretend to know me, I may return the compliment, and admit that I know you. Now what is the meaning of this sudden sympathy with Mirelle? I know you do not love her; I have eyes in my head which have long ago convinced me that you do not even like her. This outbreak of zeal for her welfare and happiness, I am led to believe, covers—as you were pleased coarsely to remark to me—some selfish aim. And that aim I can discern without difficulty. I understand,' he added with a sneer, 'that Mirelle had constituted you treasurer and agent and plenipotentiary over all her property, landed and funded and invested, with perfect liberty to deal with it as you listed, and without any one to control your proceedings and check your accounts. And *that* after her experience of how the Trampleasure family deals in trust matters! *O sancta simplicitas!*'

Orange looked at him sullenly.

'Think so if you will, but I tell you you are mistaken.' She stepped before him, barring his road, and held out her hands. 'Captain Trecarrel, I give you one chance more. Let her go. Send her to her convent. Have pity upon both her and me.' Then her rage swelled into a paroxysm; she grasped his shoulders with her strong hands, and shook him. 'Captain Trecarrel, will you be advised, will you be ruled? Do not think in your heart that ever she will be yours, and Welltown joined to Trecarrel! That will never, never be. Let her go. You alone can save her. The carriage has halted for us at the top of the hill. Now call to the postilion to turn his horses and drive back to Plymouth.'

Captain Trecarrel released himself, with a feeling of disgust at her violence and ill-breeding.

'Let us catch up the carriage, Orange,' he said coldly: 'we have dropped far behind. You are excited, and hot, and unreasonable. If you wish to hear what directions I shall give to the driver, you must wait.'

They walked on hastily, side by side, without speaking. Orange's breath was like a flame between her lips.

The post-boy had drawn up the horses at the head of the hill. As they prepared to step into the chaise, Captain Trecarrel remarked—

'She is asleep still. Bless me, she looks as if she might sleep away into death without those looking on being conscious of the change.'

Orange took her place opposite Mirelle, and Captain Trecarrel sat by the sleeper's side.

'You really wish this?' he asked of Orange.

'Yes; give the word to the post-boy,' she answered, looking him hard in the face.

'Drive straight on,' shouted the Captain; 'we are ready.'

Orange sank back in her seat and said no more. Trecarrel looked about him, and admired the richness of the scenery, as the road descended to the beautiful valley of the Tavy, rich in woods, with glimpses of granite moor ridges rising picturesquely above it, and below the little town of Tavistock, with its grey church and abbey nestling by the foaming moorland river. The scene was charming, and the Captain wished he had time to sketch it.

Presently Mirelle woke—woke with a start and shiver.

'Orange!' she said, 'you frighten me. Why do you look at me in that strange manner?'

'I did not know that I was looking at you at all,' answered Orange, and she turned away her face.

'I am cold,' said Mirelle; 'we have our backs to the sun.'

'You have been asleep, and have become chilled,' said the Captain, sympathetically. 'Let me wrap my warm cloak about your shoulders; you must not catch cold. We are now half-way to Launceston.'

Then Genefer murmured, 'The Lord put a lying spirit in the mouth of the prophets, and they said unto Ahab, Go up unto Ramoth Gilead and take it; and he went up and fell there. I cannot see; my eyes are holden. The Lord hath not spoken unto me by word or sign or revelation, and I know not if I counselled right when I said, Return.'

Nothing of interest and worthy of record occurred during the rest of the journey. Mirelle was brighter, refreshed by her sleep, and she tried to enter into conversation with the Captain, but Orange remained obdurately mute. At the gate of Launceston Trecarrel descended and offered profuse thanks to Mirelle for the drive which had saved him the expense of coaching home. The evening had fallen and it was dusk; the chaise was driven rapidly into the gate of Dolbeare, and drew up on the terrace.

The house was locked; no one now lived in it. Orange had taken the key with her to Plymouth; she handed it to Genefer, whilst the post-boy let down the steps, and she descended. Genefer went, with the key in her hand, towards the door, when suddenly she stopped, uttered a cry of terror, and fell back.

'What is the matter?' asked Orange, impatiently.

'Do'y see un? Do'y see un? There he stands.'

'Who? what? No one is there,' answered Orange in a tone of irritation. 'You foolish woman, go on.

'I see an old man in red; he be there standing with his walking-stick waving it, and signing to us not to come in. He has his hand out, as though to thrust us back. He stands in the doorway.'

'This is sheer crazy folly,' exclaimed Orange. 'Here, give me the key!' She snatched it from Genefer's hand, and thrusting her aside went forward.

Genefer turned her head and uttered another cry. Mirelle had fainted.

'She saw him too, I reckon—that man in a red coat, with the white hair and the gold-headed cane,' said the old woman. 'O Lord, enlighten me! What be the meaning of all this, I cannot tell.'

Orange threw the house door open, and the unconscious Mirelle was borne into the hall by Genefer and the post-boy, and placed in an arm-chair, where she gradually recovered.

'I'll be quick, darling,' said Genefer, 'and get a fire lighted and something warm, and I'll bring you your supper up to your own room.'

'You are over tired,' said Orange. 'Genefer is right; go to bed.'

When the Trampleasures had removed to Welltown nothing definite was settled as to where they would permanently take up their abode; the furniture and all the contents of Dolbeare had therefore been left there undisturbed, to be removed should they elect to live elsewhere. It was convenient to them to have the house in condition to receive them at any time for a short or lengthy stay as suited them. On their way to Plymouth Mirelle and Orange had spent the night there, and Genefer had attended to their requirements. Now that they had returned, the old servant's hands were full of work. She lighted the fire in the kitchen and in the dining-room, filled the kettle and set it on to boil, and began to prepare for supper. This occupied some time, during which she was unable to attend to Mirelle. When the supper was ready she brought it into the dining-room, and found Orange there seated musing by the hearth.

'How be the mistress now?' asked Grenefer.

'I do not know. I have not been upstairs.'

Genefer looked up at the pastille portrait above her head, and said, 'Him it was that I saw in the doorway with a warning wave of the hand, and he sought to bar the door entrance with the stick, that we might not come in. I durst not have passed, but when you went forward, Miss Orange, then he seemed to vanish away like smoke. I reckon the mistress saw un too, for her fainted with fright at the same moment. Did'y ever hear, now, who he might be?'

'No, I know nothing of him,' answered Orange, shortly.

'I reckon he don't come for naught,' said Genefer. 'But a veil is on my face in the reading of events, as there be on the hearts of the Jews in the study of Scripture, and till that veil be taken away I see naught plain.'

'Go about your work,' said Orange, impatiently, 'and do not trouble me with your foolish fancies.'

Genefer looked at Orange, and shook her head, and muttered, 'There be some folks like the fleece of Gideon on which the dew never falls though the grass around be wet.'

Then she prepared a tray, and carried some supper upstairs to Mirelle. 'Ah!' she continued, 'and there be others on whom the dew drops in plenty whilst all around is dry.'

She found her mistress seated in a high-backed, old-fashioned chair covered with red baize. She had her shawl wrapped about her. 'There, my pretty,' said the old woman; 'see, I've a brought you something at last.'

'Oh, Geneviève, I am very cold,' said Mirelle.

'Shall I light the fire, darling?'

'I should like it. I do not think I am well. I am exhausted, and sick at heart. Feel my hand how it shakes.'

Genefer took the little white hand between her own, stroked it, raised it to her lips and kissed it.

'You love me, Geneviève?' Mirelle lifted her large eyes and looked earnestly into the old woman's face.

'Ah, I do, I do, sure-ly.'

'I am so glad, Geneviève, because I do not think there are many who love me.'

'Do'y think it was the red man in the doorway that frightened you?' asked Genefer. 'You seed un, did you not?'

'I do not know,' answered Mirelle. 'I hardly remember what occurred. I had a sense of a great wave of terror coming over me, but what caused it I no more remember, for my consciousness went from me.'

'He've a got a kindly enough face, there be no vice in it,' said Genefer, as she knelt at the hearth and was engaged on the fire. 'I reckon he don't walk for naught; it ain't only the bad as wanders. Samuel appeared to Saul before the battle of Gilboa. Many of the saints that slept arose, and appeared in the holy city. We have Scripture to show that it be not the bad only as walks. I've a seen my mother scores of times, and her were a God-fearing woman. But father were a darning blaspheming drunkard, and I've never seen him once. I reckon the red man were a peaceable sort of a chap, and if he walks, 'tain't along of his sins, but because he be sent to fulfil the wise purposes of Heaven.'

Genefer put the poker against the bars of the grate.

'There, mistress, I hope you'll be warmer soon, but the kindling be damp and the chimney has cold air in it, and the fire won't draw kindly. Now I must go.'

'Oh, Geneviève, must you really go? I do not like to be alone, I am frightened.'

'Is it the red man you fear? Do'y think he'll walk through the room while you be lying in bed? Lord bless'y, I think naught of such spirits. It be the black devils is the chaps to scare one; I've a seed them and hunted 'em many a time.'

'No,' said Mirelle, 'I am not afraid of him. I do not know exactly what I fear, but something that I cannot describe has come over me. Oh, Geneviève, I wish that you could sleep in this room with me.'

'I don't see how to manage that, my dear. I couldn't move my bed myself up here. But you've no occasion for it, neither. There be Miss Orange close at hand, and only a door between. You ask her, and her'll leave the door open between you.'

'No, no,' said Mirelle, nervously. 'Could you fasten that door, Geneviève?'

'Which? There be but two doors, one is on to the landing, and the other into Miss Orange's bedroom.'

'I mean the latter door.'

Genefer went to it.

'I cannot fasten it. It be locked already, and the key on the other side.'

'Is there no bolt?'

'No, mistress.'

'Never mind, it cannot be helped,' with a sigh.

Then the lock was turned, the door opened, and Orange came through carrying a bolster.

'You like to lie with your head well raised. I have brought you this; you will sleep the sounder for it.'

Then she went up to Mirelle's bed and placed it with the pillows.

'Thank you, Orange. How very kind and thoughtful you are!' said Mirelle.

Orange went up to her. Orange had lost her colour, and a hard, restrained look had come over her face.

'How are you now?'

'A little better; not much. I feel very cold.'

'It is heart,' said Orange, 'that ails you. That will stop some day—or night. Stop in a moment when least expected.' And without another word she went back through her door and re-locked it.

'Shall I unpack your box, mistress?' asked the old woman. 'It won't do for you to stoop. It might bring the swimming in your head again. It is only for me to stay up a bit later to finish the housework.'

'Thank you, dear, kind Geneviève. I am much obliged, I shall be very glad of it.'

Genefer uncorded and unlocked the trunk and removed from it what she thought would be necessary for the night.

'Shall I bring out this Christ on the cross?' she asked, holding up the crucifix Herring had bought for his bride.

'Oh, please do so. I shall be glad to have it.'

'Ah!' said the old woman, 'if the fear and sickness of heart come over you again, you can look to that and take comfort. I be not that set against images such as this, that I would forbid and destroy them. Since you've been to Welltown I've a looked on this here many scores of times, and it have done me a deal of good, it have.'

Then she planted the crucifix in the middle of a small table at the head of

167

the bed, between a couple of wax lights that were burning there.

Mirelle shivered. 'Oh, Geneviève! what have you done? Do you know that with us we put a crucifix and candles in that way at the head of a bed where some one is lying dead?'

'Let be,' said Genefer. 'Sleep is a figure of death, and if you cannot sleep under the cross you are not fit to die under it. Remember what Miss Orange said. You suffer from the heart, and it may stop at any hour; so be always ready.' She went again to the hearth. 'Drat the fire, it won't burn, leastwise not readily; there be too much cold air in the flue. There, mistress, now I must go; I've my work to do downstairs.'

'May I have a rushlight for the night, Geneviève?'

'My dear, there be none in the house; I'd go gladly and fetch you one, but the shops be all shut in the town. There, good night, and God be with you.'

'Where do you sleep, Geneviève?'

'At the far end of the house, up the other flight of stairs.'

'If I should want you? If I should call in the night?' Mirelle looked anxiously, pleadingly at her.

'My darling, it would be no good. I should never hear. But what do that matter? Miss Orange be close at hand, and you've but to call if you feel ill, and her'll run and wake me up, and I'll go for the doctor fast as lightning, so there, don't'y fear any more.'

Mirelle sighed. 'Give me a kiss, Geneviève, before you go.'

'With all my heart, precious!' and the old woman kissed her fondly on the cheek, and then raised and kissed both her hands in succession.

Then Genefer left. It was not possible for her to tarry longer with Mirelle. There was much that had to be done: the supper things to be removed and washed up, some kindling to be got ready for the fire next morning; the kitchen fire to be put out, and a little tidying to be done in the parlour and the hall. Genefer would have enough to do next morning, getting breakfast ready, and she would leave nothing till then that she could possibly get done that night.

Whilst she was in the dining-room clearing away the supper things, she looked hard at the pastille portrait.

'Whatever did the old man mean by walking, and standing in the doorway with that warning gesture?'

She stood in front of the picture for some time, trying to decipher something in it which escaped her. At last, hopeless of discovering what she sought, she resumed her work.

'There, there!' she said, 'I've been wasting the one bit of candle I have, and her'll hardly last me out all I have to do. Whatever be hidden now from me, the day will bring forth.'

After the old woman had finished the washing-up in the kitchen and had extinguished that fire and raked out the fire in the parlour, she went into the hall, which was littered with packages, boxes, trunks, cloaks, and calashes. Genefer disliked disorder, and she set to work putting the sundry articles into some sort of order, though the next day all would again be removed to the carriage for the continuation of the return journey to Welltown.

'I wonder what time of night it be!' she said, as she looked up at the clock. 'Twelve! But no, sure it cannot be. Her's not ticking. Her's standing still. To be sure, her's not been wounded up for ever so long. Loramussy! the candle will never last me out. I shall have to go to bed in the dark, and that ain't pleasant where there be spirits of dead men walking. But'—she shook herself—'is that seemly of thee, Genefer Benoke, to be afeared of spirits? The Lord is my light and my salvation, whom shall I fear? The Lord is the strength of my life, of whom shall I be afraid?'

Genefer's confidence was somewhat shaken by hearing a door opened, and by seeing a white figure on the stairs, slowly descending.

'Lord, mistress!' she said, after she had recovered from the first shock of alarm, when she recognised Mirelle; 'sure enough you did give me a turn.'

Mirelle was in her long white nightdress, her dark hair was unbound, and fell over her shoulders. The white, delicate feet were bare.

'What be the matter, darling?'

Mirelle took each step on the stair hesitatingly, with foot poised before her, as though feeling in the air, before she lowered it. She descended in this way very leisurely, as one walking in a dream, or one blind, groping the way in an unknown place. Her hand was on the banister, and the bar trembled.

She reached the landing, and stood under the clock. She made no attempt to descend farther.

'Oh, Geneviève, the fire is gone out.'

'I reckon the wood were damp,' said the old woman. 'It be too late, and not possible to light it again now.'

'And the candles are flickering in their sockets.'

'There is not another in the house. Look at mine.'

'It will be so dark.'

'Do not be afraid. The Lord will give you light.'

'It will be so cold.'

'You will be warm in bed.'

'O no! it is colder there than outside.'

She remained without speaking, waiting for Genefer to say something, but the old woman offered no remark, not knowing what to say.

Still she stood there, hesitating, and the banister rattled under her hand laid on it.

'There, there!' said Genefer, 'lie down and shut your eyes, and you will soon be asleep.'

'I cannot sleep.'

She still stood there, irresolute.

'Is the fire burning in the parlour? I should like to go in there, and sit there.'

'I've just put him out.' 'Then—

that in the kitchen.'

'He's out likewise. There, there, go to bed like a good dear. There is no help—it must be.'

'Geneviève, I asked Mr. John Herring to send you away. You frightened me. I am very sorry. Will you forgive me for doing so?'

'To be sure I will. I am not one to bear malice.'

'Do you really think, Geneviève, that he is alive?'

'I do. I cannot doubt it.'

'Oh, promise me, if ever you see him, and I not, tell him'—she paused —'tell him that now I wish, with all my heart, I had loved him as he deserved.'

Then she went upstairs again, in the same slow, reluctant manner, step by step, ascending backward, feeling each step behind her with her bare foot before planting it, and raising herself to the higher level, and she kept her eyes fixed on Genefer as though dreading to lose sight of her. At last Mirelle's hand, feeling behind her, touched the latch of her door, and the chill of the metal sent a shiver through her.

Slowly, very slowly, she pressed the door open behind her, walking backwards still, with a sad despairing look in her large dark eyes fixed on Genefer.

And Genefer, standing below, said, 'Sweetheart, go to your bed, and, MAY YOU REST IN PEACE!'

171

CHAPTER LIX.

DIVIDING THE SPOILS.

'Never was more shocked in my life!' said Captain Trecarrel; 'I really have not recovered it yet. So young, so beautiful, so good! and you, my sweet Orange, I observe, are greatly overcome. It does you credit; it does, upon my life.'

Captain Trecarrel was seated in the parlour at Dolbeare with Orange; the latter was looking haggard and wretched. 'And it was heart that did it,' said the Captain; 'I always said that heart was her weak point, and that it must be economised to the utmost, spared all excitement, everything distressing. There has always been that transparent look about her flesh that is a sure sign of the heart being wrong. Poor angel! I have no doubt in the world that she was greatly tried. She has not been happy ever since she came to England; one thing or another has risen up to distress her, circumstances have conspired to keep her in incessant nervous tension. She felt the death of poor John Herring severely; that alone was enough to kill her. Do not take on so much, Orange; there is moderation in all things, even in sorrow for the dead.'

'Leave me alone,' said Orange, hoarsely. 'Do not notice me.'

'I see this painful occurrence has shaken you,' continued Captain Trecarrel. 'I knew you regarded her; I had no idea that you loved her. Indeed ____'

'Leave me alone,' said Orange, emphatically.

'Well, well! When will be the funeral?'

'To-morrow.'

'I shall certainly attend, to show the last tribute of respect to one whom I greatly esteemed. Indeed I may say that next to you, Orange, I never admired any woman so much. She has taught us one lesson, poor thing, and that is not to trifle with the heart, which is a most susceptible organ, and must be guarded against strong feeling and excitement. Do not be so troubled about this matter, Orange; it is bad for the health, over much sorrow debilitates the constitution. You are really not looking yourself. Think that every cloud has its silver lining, and this fleeting affliction, I make no scruple to affirm, is trimmed throughout with gold. Have you reversed it? Have you studied the other side? Have you looked into matters at all?'

'What matters?'

'Well, to put it broadly, pecuniary matters. One is reluctant to advert to such things at such a solemn time, but it is necessary. The sweet luxury of grief cannot be indulged in till these concerns are settled, and they considerably accentuate or moderate it. You and I, Orange, are practical persons: we feel for what we have lost, but we do not let slip the present or overlook the future. You are her nearest of kin, and therefore of course everything she had will fall to you. By the greatest good luck her husband predeceased, and Welltown came to her, and from her will doubtless pass to you. Beside Welltown, what was she worth?'

'I do not know—I do not care,' answered Orange, in a tone of mingled impatience and indifference.

'This will not do, Orange,' said Captain Trecarrel; 'you really must not succumb. Good taste imposes its limits on sorrow as on joy. If you come in for ten thousand pounds you do not dance and shout, and if you lose a friend you do not sink into the abyss of sulky misery—that is, if you make any pretence to good breeding. I know what a sensible, practical girl you are. Come, pluck up heart and help me to look into her concerns. I have done my best, my very best, for you so far, and I will not desert you now. The moment I heard of the event I flew to your assistance, I offered my aid, and I have been invaluable to you. You cannot dispute it. But for me there might have been an inquest, which would have been offensive to your delicacy of sentiment. I explained to the doctor her constitution, and the troubles she has gone through; how she felt her husband's sudden death, the languor that has since oppressed her, her fainting fits, the swoon into which she fell after her exhausting journey; and he saw at once that heart was at the bottom of it all. I settled with the undertaker, saw to everything, made every arrangement, and you have not been troubled in the least. I even went after the milliner about your mourning. You cannot deny that I have been of service to you, and I am ready to do more. All that is nothing: now comes the most trying and difficult task of all—the settlement of her affairs; but I am ready to undertake that also, to save my dear Orange trouble, only I ask, as a preliminary, that all the requisite information shall be placed at my disposal.'

'Later,' said Orange, uneasily; 'after the funeral.'

'No,' answered Captain Trecarrel, 'not after the funeral, but now. My time is valuable. I shall have to go to Exeter in three days, and I should like to have everything ready to take with me. If there be a will, which I do not suppose there is, I will prove it for you. If there be not, I will obtain letters of administration for you. You must really let me know what her estate was worth. Have you the means of ascertaining?'

'I do not know.'

'But you must know, or rather you must put me in the way of ascertaining. Have you looked whether there is a will?'

'No, I have not.'

'Have you got her desk?'

'It is upstairs.'

'Bring it down, and we will overhaul it together.'

Orange rose and left the room. She returned a few minutes later, with the large desk that had belonged to Mr. Strange, and after his death had been appropriated by Mirelle. Mirelle had removed from it all his Portuguese letters, tied them in bundles and put them away, and had transferred to it her own treasures from a school writing-desk full to overflowing. It was a strange thing that this desk was thus explored in search of a will at so small an interval of time since we saw John Herring seated at it, at the opening of this story.

'This is the sort of thing I detest,' said the Captain. 'It jars with one's feelings and vulgarises bereavement. However, it does not become us to give way to our emotions, we must do our duty. Give me the key.'

He unlocked the desk, and turned over the contents; he removed many articles and placed them on the table. What trifles were there!—trifles that had been collected at school and were preserved as treasures, each made precious by some innocent association and sunny memory. A little book in which her school companions had inscribed verses and signed their names. Wrapped up in silver paper and tied with white silk, a lock of hair from the head of Marie de la Meillerie, cut on the day of her first Communion. In a pill-box a raisin out of Mirelle's birthday cake, many years old. Some lace-edged pictures of saints, spangled red, and blue, and gold with foil stars, a medal of Notre-Dame de Bon Secours; some feathers off a pet bullfinch that had died and cost many tears, a twig of blessed palm, John Herring's notes, and some little presents he had made her—but not one relic of Captain Trecarrel—all such had been burned on her marriage, she had kept them till then. Also a little deal box in which, softly nested in cotton-wool, was a glass peacock with spun glass tail—a memorial of one happy day spent at the house of the Countess La Gaye, who had taken Mirelle and her daughters to see a glass-blower, and the man had made the peacock under their eyes, and had presented it to Mirelle. All this rubbish Captain Trecarrel tossed aside carelessly. If it ever had any value, it had it only to her who could appreciate those trifles no more. Then he pounced, with trembling hand, on a paper in John Herring's handwriting statement of the property of the Countess Mirelle Garcia de Cantalejo; and with it a much larger paper in many folds. He opened this latter, glanced at it, and tossed it aside with an expression of disgust. It was a pedigree of the family of Garcia de Cantalejo with heraldic blazonings. The smaller paper soon engrossed his whole attention; Captain Trecarrel's eyes opened very wide. John Herring's confession was not there. Mirelle had destroyed it, lest it should ever be seen by any one but herself. She had, however, preserved the statement.

'My dear Orange!—my dear, dear Orange!' his voice shook with emotion and excitement. 'I had no idea that the lining was so warm and so rich. There are the West Wyke mortgages, there is a silver lead mine, about which I knew nothing—well, I was aware some time ago that he was paddling in something of the sort near Ophir, but I did not know that it was being worked; when I heard of it, it was not begun. Then there are uncut diamonds. Bless my soul! uncut diamonds! How did they escape the fingers of your excellent father, I wonder? Where can they be? Oh, I see, at the bank. We must take out letters of administration to authorise you to withdraw and realise. Why, Orange! my dear, dear, dear Orange,' he put his hand under the table, took that of Miss Trampleasure, and pressed it with fervent affection; 'the barrier that has stood between us has fallen. Happiness is in view before us. You will forgive and forget any little past lovers' quarrels. *Amantium iræ amoris integratio est*, as the syntax says. Let me tott all up as well as I can. Welltown is worth six hundred nett, as far as I can judge, and it is unencumbered. Then there are your five thousand, which will bring in, say, two hundred and fifty. It is impossible for me to estimate the value of Mirelle's own property, as the silver lead mine is only now beginning to give dividends, I suppose—I see by the paper that money has been sunk, and there is no entry of return, but then Upaver is quite a new affair. What it is worth I cannot conjecture. Then there are the West Wyke mortgages, and the uncut diamonds, and I suppose money in the bank. The estate must be worth at least a thousand per annum, without including Welltown. My dear, dear, dear Orange, my heart overflows with affection. I will tell you, Orange, what will be the best plan of all for both of us. Let us get a special licence and be married at the earliest time possible, privately, of course, because of the affliction under which you are suffering, and then I can manage all the matter of Mirelle's estate with the utmost simplicity, as my own. It will save a world of trouble, and possibly some expense. By Jove! this is not all. We had left out of our calculation the set of diamonds. Where is it? Oh, here it is in its *étui* on the other side of the desk. Orange, do look at the stones! they are magnificent. They must be worth a great deal of money. I am no judge of stones, but these strike my uninitiated eye as being of the purest water—not a tinge of yellow, not a flaw in them. I can see this, Orange, that our income is likely to be some two thousand a year. I could cry tears of joy at the thought. Did you ever hear anything so ridiculous as the supposition that John Herring had committed suicide with this set of diamonds in his pocket? The thing is psychologically impossible. With such a source of wealth in one's pocket one would begin to live; all previous existence would be tadpolism, now only would one stretch out legs and arms and begin to jump. My dear, dear Orange, I do believe that you and I are only now about to sip the nectar of life. Here—try on these jewels.'

'I had rather not,' said Orange, shrinking back.

'I insist. I want to see you in them. Lord bless you! they never could become that pale little thing; colour, warmth, flesh and life are wanted to carry this. Here, Orange, let me try it on.'

He rose to put the diamond chain about her neck, when a hand interposed and grasped it.

Trecarrel and Orange looked round, startled, and saw John Herring standing before them, with hard, bitter face, very pale, with contracted brows. He had entered the room without their hearing him. The Captain had been too much engrossed in his discoveries to have ear for his footfall on the carpet, and Orange too abstracted in her own gloomy thoughts.

At the sight of Herring, Trecarrel drew back, and his jaw fell. He looked at Herring, then at Orange, then at the diamonds, and, lastly, at the schedule of Mirelle's property.

'By heavens!' he gasped. 'Confound it! you alive! Then Orange is only worth five thousand.'

Orange had recoiled into a corner, blank, trembling, speechless.

Herring was perfectly collected.

'Put everything down,' he said in hard tones. 'Do not lay finger on anything again. Leave the house at once.' He looked at the Captain with contempt and anger.

'And you, Orange Trampleasure, already engaged in dividing the spoils of the dead before she is laid in her grave! You will find a carriage at the gate. Rejoin your mother at Welltown, and leave me in the house alone with Genefer and—my wife. I cannot suffer another presence here.'

He gathered the little scattered trifles together, the lock of hair, the raisin, the glass peacock, the tinsel pictures, with soft and reverent touch, and placed all together in the desk. The jewels he re-laid in their *étui*, and relegated it to its proper compartment. Then he locked up the desk. His face was cold, collected, with hard lines about the mouth, and a hard look in the eyes, in which no sign of a tear was manifest. He removed the desk to a shelf in the cabinet, then he went out and ascended the stairs.

At the sound of his step, a door at the head of the staircase opened, and Genefer came out, with her eyes red, and tears glittering on her cheek.

'It be you, to last, Master John. I knew it. I knew you wasn't dead. God be praised! Even out of the belly of the whale; when the waters compass me about, even to the soul; when the depth hath closed me round about, and the weeds are wrapped about my head. I will say, Salvation is of the Lord.'

Herring was about to pass her, but she stayed him, barring the door, looking hard into his face.

'Oh, Master John! you must not go in looking like that, as the fleece of Gideon without dew. Stay and let me tell you, afore you see the sweet flower of God, His white lily, what was her message to you, the last words her uttered in this world. Her was standing where I be now, and her said to me:

"Promise me, if ever you see him, to tell him that I wish with all my heart I had loved him as he deserves." That were the olive leaf in the mouth of the dove as her flew back to the ark.'

The old woman opened the door and went forward, leading the way, with her arms uplifted, saying, 'The dove found no rest for the sole of her foot, and she returned into the ark, for the waters were on the face of the whole earth: then He put forth His hand, and took her, and pulled her in unto Him into the ark.' As the old woman said these last words, she touched the crucifix and the right, transfixed hand of the figure on it.

The white blinds were down in the room, the atmosphere was sweet with the scent of violets. At the head of the little bed was a table covered with a linen cloth, and the crucifix between bunches of white flowers and lighted wax candles was on it. Upon the bed lay Mirelle, her face as the purest wax, and a wreath of white and purple violets round her head, woven by the loving hands of old Genefer. The hands, contrary to the usual custom, were crossed over the breast. Genefer had seen this on a monument 'of the old Romans,' and she had thus arranged the hands of Mirelle, thinking it would be right so for her.

Herring stood by the bed looking at the pure face. Then he signed with one hand to Genefer to leave. The old woman went out softly. Herring still looked, and drawing forth a little case opened it and took out a sprig of white heath and laid it in the bosom of his dead wife.

'Mirelle! once you refused it when I offered it you, once you refused it when offered you by Trecarrel, now you will keep and carry with you into eternity my good luck which I now give you.'

CHAPTER LX.

INTRODUCTORY.

Several weeks had passed. John Herring was back at West Wyke, grave, calm, with a gentle expression in his face and a far-off look in his eyes. The hardness and bitterness had gone, never to return. The Snow Bride would not freeze him to ice. He, in time, would thaw away like her. On his first return to West Wyke he had come back with blasted hopes, on his second with dislocated faith. Now he returned with recovered moral balance, not indeed hopeful, for hope is a delusion of youth, but able to look life in the face without a sneer.

Cicely received him with her usual brightness and sympathy. It was always pleasant to see her kind, sweet face, and to know what a good and honest heart beat in her bosom.

Herring had never been to her other than uncommunicative, partly out of natural modesty, partly because they were out of harmony over Mirelle. But Cicely had a woman's curiosity, and would not be left in the dark as to what had taken place; and she felt real sympathy for John Herring, only she did not know how to exhibit it, because she did not know what course it should take. So she put to him questions, and with tact drew from him the entire story.

'Where does she lie, John?' she asked in her soft tones, full of tender feeling for his sorrow. They were sitting together in the porch, looking out on the old walled garden, with its honesty, and white rocket, and love-lies-bleeding all ablow. 'Have you laid her in Launceston churchyard, or removed her to Welltown?'

He shook his head. 'No, Cicely. Neither under the shadow of Launceston church, nor exposed to the winds and roar of Boscastle. She lies in the sunny cemetery of the Sacré Coeur.'

Cicely said nothing. Indeed, neither spoke for some time. Presently, however, Cicely, who had laid her needlework in her lap, and had rested her folded hands on it, and was looking dreamily across the garden, said, 'Mirelle was your ideal, John.'

'She *is* my ideal, Cicely.'

Miss Battishill looked round at him. She was very pretty, with her copper-gold hair, and the reflection of the sunlight in the garden illumining her sweet face of the most delicate white and purest pink. 'I remember your speaking to me—almost when first I knew you, about Mirelle as your ideal, and I thought what you said was extravagant and unreal. But I was in fault. There was no exaggeration, and all was real to you.'

'It was, and is so still.'

'Now, tell me the truth, honestly, cousin, does the possession of such an ideal in the heart conduce to happiness?'

'On the contrary, it saddens.'

'Then why do you not shut your eyes to such alluring but unsatisfying fancies? Why are you not satisfied with what *is*, instead of sighing after what *may be*?'

'Cicely, it seems to me that the world is divided between those with ideals and those without. When I say without, I mean that the great bulk of mankind are, as you say, content with things as they are. They are without ambition after the perfect, they are satisfied with the defective. Such men put forth their hands, and without effort gather happiness. They ask for nothing very high, and certainly nothing above them. They are vulgarly happy, enjoying what is on their level and attained without effort. But there are others who are not thus easily satisfied. They form in their minds an ideal from which every imperfection is cast off, and the formation of this ideal in their hearts deals it its death-wound. The ideal is the ever-unattainable, and if happiness consists in obtaining the desired, happiness can never be theirs, because the ideal can never be reached. Hope also is killed along with happiness, for how can you hope for the unobtainable? The ideal may be of various sorts—it may be sought in moral, social, political, religious perfection; in Woman, in the State, in the Church, in Art; but is always pursued with disappointment—I had almost said with despair. When I was a child, I was told by my nurse that under the root of the rainbow lay a golden bowl, and many is the rainbow I have run after in hopes of finding the golden chalice from which could be quaffed immortality. As I grew older and always failed, I found that the rainbow moved before me as I advanced, and that the cup of supreme felicity could never be pressed by my lips. That is the picture of all idealists. We have given up every hope of attaining the Iris we look on, but we still follow it.'

'I think yours is a sad story, John.'

'Perhaps so, but I do not know. Mirelle has been my ideal, and therefore unattainable.'

'But, John, suppose she had really loved you, and been everything you could wish as a wife—you would have been happy.'

'I should have been happy—yes. But my ideal would have died. I remember a story that Genefer—by the way, you do not know her—my old nurse told me many years ago of a man of Trevalga, who saw a pixy, a beautiful fairy who haunted the glen and waterfall of S. Kneighton. He saw her when she was bathing, and took away her white garment, and refused to restore it till she allowed him to kiss her lips. She wept and pleaded, but in vain. Then she suffered him to draw her to him and to touch her lips, but the touch of mortal flesh withered her. She shrivelled like a faded rose, and lost all beauty, and became as a wizened hag. And he went from his mind and drowned himself in the Kieve. I cannot conceive of Mirelle other than one far, far above and distant from me. It is possible, had things been as you say, that I might have discovered imperfections.'

'Of course she had her imperfections,' interrupted Cicely, with a slight touch of impatience in her tone. 'I do not wish to say a word that may wound you, but, my dear John, nothing human is perfect, and certainly Mirelle had her short-comings apparent enough to me.'

'Then, better a thousand times that things should be as they are, that these imperfections should not have been seen by me; and now, I know they are swallowed up in a faultless splendour. If Heaven gave me my choice, I would choose this.'

'Do you mean seriously to tell me that you would not have Mirelle restored, and restored to be yours entirely?'

'I would not. I had rather have my unapproachable ideal shining down upon me from afar, than have my ideal dissolve in my arms into the commonplace. The ship sails by the star but never attains to it. I can look up, and I am content. I ask for nothing more.'

'This frame of mind is to me inexplicable. It is unworthy of a man of reason to strive for the unreachable. When a person of sense sees that what he or she has wished is not to be had, that person makes an effort and accommodates herself to circumstances.' She coloured a little.

'That is to say—some weary of pursuing an ideal, and settle themselves down to enjoy what they can obtain. I can quite understand that; and perhaps it is the most practical course, but it is, to some, impossible.'

'But that is the most—it is the only, sensible course. The other offers a mere treadmill round of duties, without hope to spur you on, and happiness to reward you.'

'No doubt you are right; and yet it is impossible to some. I have set up pure and perfect womanhood as my ideal; but others have ideals of different nature. The young politician starts with an ideal of a perfect commonwealth before him, and he is sanguine of redressing grievances, of elevating politics to a noble patriotic passion instead of mean party rivalry. But after a while he finds that every reform brings in fresh evils, and, if it does away with some wrongs, it inflicts others; he finds that it is impossible to be patriotic without partisanship, and that those whom he strives to raise are unworthy of being raised. I believe the leaders of the Revolution in France were earnest men with their ideal before them, and, striving after a perfect state of liberty and fraternity, they called up a Reign of Terror. I saw once an enthusiast who had taken to educate a pig; he taught it letters, he washed the beast clean, and dressed it in a coat, but, when left to itself, it wallowed in the next mire and forgot its alphabet. I have no doubt that a young curate starts on his sacred duties with the sincere hope and belief that he will do good: he preaches with earnestness, thinking to waken the religious sense of his people, he establishes schools to instruct the young, and presently finds that all he has done is absolutely useless—the people will not be regenerated, his sermons are profitless, and his educated children read only vicious literature. It is the same —— But I see I weary you.'

'I do not understand you.'

They were silent awhile.

Presently Cicely said: 'John, do you not think your own weakness may be at the bottom of all the trouble you have met with? I do not speak with any intention to be unkind. You will allow that.'

Herring thought a moment. 'I do not know, Cicely, that I could have acted other than I have, and been true to my conscience. I might have taken the selfish line, and cast aside those responsibilities which seemed to me to be forced upon me, and, no doubt, then I should have been light-hearted and boyish to the present moment, laughing, shooting, riding, spending money, a careless young officer without much thought of the morrow. But I had rather have my sorrows and walk uprightly. I am better for having an ideal and following it, though I shall never catch it up.'

Cicely did not pursue the subject: she stooped over her work, took it up, and averting her pretty face said, as the colour mantled her white throat and deepened in her rosy cheek, 'John, you have been candid with me: I will be equally frank with you. I will make a confession to you.' She hesitated a moment, and then said, 'Mr. Harmless-Simpleton has asked me to be his wife.'

'I wish you joy with all my heart, dear Cicely,' said Herring, warmly. 'He is a good, well-intentioned, amiable man, with whom you are sure to be happy.'

'Vulgarly happy,' said Cicely, drily.

Herring coloured. 'I beg your pardon. I meant no disparagement when I used that term. I meant only ordinarily happy, happy as the buttercups, and the birds and bees, as all nature that is content with the place God has given it, and the sunshine and sweet air that surround it. Why should you not be so? It is no privilege to have an ever-aching void in the heart, to be ever stretching after the moon. You will be happy in a sphere where you will do good and be beloved. When do you intend to be married?'

'I do not know. There is no occasion for delay, and there is nothing to precipitate matters. But now—when I am married and settled into the Vicarage at Tawton, what is to become of that queer Joyce? Is she to come with me?'

'I—I!' Joyce was there in the door to answer for herself. 'Wherever the maister be, there be I too. He sed as how he'd never wear no stockings more but what I'd knit; and you wouldn't have he go barefoot?'

John Herring turned his head, and looked at Joyce.

'You had better remain with Miss Cicely. I do not want you.'

'I will not,' answered Joyce, resolutely. 'I go with you.'

'Then, I dare say, Genefer will find work for you on the farm, or in the house at Welltown. But you will not be so comfortable or happy as here.'

'I care not,' said the girl. 'I must follow you. I belongs to you. You bought me of vaither for shining gold. No, Miss Cicely, I follow the maister.'

'Go your ways,' said Cicely: 'you are each of you, in your several ways, idealists, and each following the unattainable.'

'And now, beginning life,' said Herring, 'all that has gone before is introductory to the real life; a rough and painful initiation into the axioms on which the problem will have to be worked out. We know now where we stand, and which is the direction in which we must set our faces, to plod on our way forward, hopeless indeed, but still, conscientiously forward.'